TYNESSA PRESENTS

TYNESSA

Text TYNESSA PRESENTS
to 22828 to join our mailing list

To submit a manuscript for our review
email us at
Tynessapublications@gmail.com

ABOUT THE AUTHOR

To keep an update of my upcoming releases, be sure to follow me on my social media.

Facebook: Tynessa Unbreakable Watson

Facebook group: Tynessa's Unbreakable Reading Group and We Are Unbreakable Reading Group.

Instagram: author_tynessa and tynessapublications

Website: Authortynessa.net

SYNOPSIS

Eliza Brown, known as La-La, is a beautiful seventeen-year-old that is madly in love with her much older boyfriend, Alonso Davis. Despite how her mother feels about her relationship with him, Eliza feels nothing or no one could tear their love apart, not even Nicole, Alonso's bitter baby mama. Alonso is one of the hoods finest. He doesn't only have good looks and money, but he seems to be everything Eliza's young heart desires in a man, but will she be ready for the heartache that comes along with dating a not only much experienced man, but a man whose life is full of drama as well?

Chyna Wilson might be only eighteen, but she knows all about heartaches and pain. With Clarence Thomas now in her life, he shows her affection that no one has ever shown her before. Immediately, Chyna finds herself comfortable enough to forget a night she deeply regrets—a night she never wants to be brought up again, not even to Clarence. However, Chyna isn't the only one with a secret. Clarence has one, too, and when it's brought to light, it will have Chyna questioning his true feelings for her, as well as his loyalty. Will the secrets be strong enough to rip these two lovebirds apart, or will their true feelings for one another conquer it all?

At the age of eighteen, Zola Mitchell feels she has the perfect relationship with Alonso's little brother, Prince Davis. He's a great provider and from day one, Prince had never hidden how he felt about her. Zola makes it a point to rub her picture-perfect relationship in her friends faces every chance she gets, but is her and Prince's relationship really picture perfect, or is it all a fairytale?

In Love Never Felt So Right, this group will show you how beautiful being in love might seem, but when it comes to the drama that sometimes follows, you just have to make sure you're ready for the heartache that it might bring.

I

Eliza Brown

"Who really cares that I'm only seventeen? I love him, and it ain't a doggone thing that you or anyone else can say to change that." I expressed, daring not to use any profanity when speaking to my mama. No matter how hard or much we argued, I would never be bold enough to stand up and curse her out. Not because I had just that much respect for her, but because it would result in me getting my ass beat.

I might've been two months away from my eighteenth birthday, but that didn't mean shit to Erika White.

"Yeah, it might not be shit I can do about it, but I bet if he pull up in front of *this* house, I'll be calling the police on his ass." She paused, looking as if she was daring me to retort something back. When I didn't, she continued on with, "You so fucking grown La-La, and I'm sick of your ass! Since you met that old bastard you done start smelling your damn self."

I sucked my teeth and rolled my eyes hard at her, turning my attention back outside. I had been posted at the screen door, staring outside and waiting for my phone to ring, when my mama walked into the living room and started talking her shit to me. It didn't take a rocket scientist to know why I was standing here, and she knew firsthand that I was about to leave and meet up with my boyfriend, Alonso, since it was clear that he couldn't pull up to my house and pick me up.

My mama hated Alonso with a passion, and I guess to some, she had every reason to. I mean, the brother was eight years older than me. Yes, while I was seventeen, he was twenty-five. But Alonso and I, we didn't see an age difference. Well, let me rephrase that, *I* didn't see an age difference. I saw two people that were madly in love, and to me, that was all that mattered.

"Why you always trying to be dramatic for no reason, ma? That man doesn't even be thinking about you, but you stay checking for him. Like, you always threatening to call the police on him, and for what?"

"For what?" My mama yelled with her eyes bucked, glaring at me like she was about to rush over and beat my ass. "Any nigga his age that's fucking with a seventeen-year-old deserves to be in jail. That shit ain't normal, La-La, but you're too fucking dickmatized to see that. I tell you one mothafuckin' thing, your hot ass better not pop up in here with no gotdamn baby, because the minute you come to me hollering about you pregnant by that old fucker, I'm beating your ass and killing his."

This time, I blew out an irritated breath and didn't bother saying anything back, because on the real, I didn't even want to argue with her. She did this every single time I got ready to leave out the house. Whether I was going to meet up with Alonso or not, she fussed, thinking I was. It was becoming redundant, and whether she liked it or not, I always left anyways.

I will say this, though; I was always sure to have my ass in the house at midnight on the weekends and eleven on a school night. If I didn't, I would've been locked out. I tried to be grown and stay out passed curfew once, and I was kicked out for almost two months.

Luckily, my grandma was able to talk my mama into letting me move back in.

My mama made sure to warn me to never try that again, because the next time, she didn't care where I stayed, I wasn't staying back in her house. I'll never forget her words, *'La-La, if you wanted to live under my roof, you would've been home when you were supposed to instead of being out in the streets doing only God knows what.'*

I guess what she said was true.

That night, I was at a party and that shit was jumping, but, I ended up leaving there around eleven when Alonso came there and picked me up. I had forgotten all about my curfew, and it was also the night Alonso and I took our relationship to the next level. It wasn't the level I wanted it to be on, but it was passed the kissing and touching we were doing at the time. *Gosh.* I remember that night like it was yesterday, and just the thought of it caused a smile to grace my face.

However, just as it appeared, it vanished due to me being snatched out my thoughts when my mama shouted, "You think this shit is funny?"

"Ma..." I jerked my body around to look at her as her carton of Newport Cigarettes hit my leg. "You play too much. I wasn't even laughing at you."

"You better not have been. Now bring me my damn cigarettes."

Doing as she demanded, I picked the box up and took them to her. She snatched it from me, and I rolled my eyes. It was at the same time my phone was ringing. Being that I knew it was Alonso, I quickly grabbed it from my back pocket and answered. My mama knew it was him, too, and her dramatic self started really fussing, making it a point to yell extra loud so he could hear her.

"I'm coming out now!" I yelled over her and then hung up in his face, praying he didn't hear her threatening to have him locked up. Taking one last look at her, I told her that wasn't even called for before storming out, ignoring her threatening to call the police on Alonso. She had been singing the same song since she found out about him, so I had become accustomed to the noise she was spitting.

I walked to the next block from my street where Alonso was in his car waiting for me. When I got inside and closed the door, I smiled and leaned over to kiss him. He would usually lean over to meet me halfway, and when he didn't and I was forced to kiss his jaw, I knew something was wrong.

As he pulled off like a bat out of hell, I asked, "What's wrong?"

"Put your seatbelt on, shawty."

Okay, now I definitely knew something was wrong, because Alonso only called me shawty when he was pissed about something. Usually, it would be, baby, bae, lil' mama or baby girl.

"What did I do, Lonso?" I pressed my lips together as I put on my seatbelt. "Or who done pissed you off and you about to take it out on me?"

The words he mumbled caused me to jump and look behind me. Alonso had his six-year-old son in the car. So, I knew I wasn't about to get an answer out of him right now, and seeing his son back there made me believe that maybe his baby mama had pissed him off.

After all, she was truly a bitter bitch.

"Hey, AJ... How are you?"

He smiled, displaying the huge gap from his two missing teeth being gone. "Good."

I smiled back. He was truly a cutie, and looked every bit of his daddy.

"That's good. So, you spending the day with daddy, today, huh?"

"We're going to get ice cream and a toy. You coming with us?"

I opened my mouth to tell him I guess I was, being that his dad had picked me up before they went, but those words didn't get a chance to come out due to Alonso answering for me. He told AJ, "Nah. I'm about to drop you back off at home, and we're going to get that ice cream and toy tomorrow. Okay?"

My face scrunched up as my lips parted. I wanted to ask why, but again, I knew he wasn't going to tell me. So, I only shook my head, turned back around in my seat and faced straight ahead.

I tried to keep my eyes fixed on the road, but I couldn't. They kept shifting over to Alonso. Even when I had taken my phone out my purse to text my best friends, Zola and Chyna, in our group chat, *best bitches forever*, every once in a while, they would find their way back to him.

La-La: I don't know what in the hell is wrong with Lonso. He is sitting here with a fucking attitude. Like, I didn't even do shit to him.

Chyna: Ask him what in the hell is wrong with him. Ask him if he on his period since he's acting like a bitch.

La-La: Shut the hell up, Chy, before you get cursed the hell out... You always saying something stupid, and he's not going to tell me anything because AJ is in the car with us. We're taking him home.

Zola: Hold the hell up, La-La... He's taking you to that girl's house, knowing she don't like you?

When Zola texted back, I just put my phone back in my purse without replying. Zola was my girl and everything, but sometimes she tried acting like her shit didn't stink. She was dating Alonso's little brother—who wasn't that much younger than Alonso. Prince was twenty-three. Yes, Zola was already eighteen, but still... She was dating a man older as well. So, to me, she couldn't talk because all three of us were into men older than us.

"Come on, AJ. Get out on this side," Alonso said after he pulled in front of his baby mama's house and threw his car in park.

"Bye, La-La." The sadness in AJ's voice was in full force, and I felt bad. No, I didn't know for sure if I was the cause of Alonso's change of plans or what, but I felt bad because I could tell that baby wanted his ice cream and toy his dad had promised him.

"Bye, baby. I'll see you next time. Okay?"

"Okay." He crawled out of the door that Alonso was holding open for him. As they walked up to the house, I took my phone out my purse to read all the messages my girls had left in the group chat. They had stopped talking about me and started talking about their men, Prince and Alonso's homeboy, Clarence.

I was in the middle of texting my girls back when, all of a sudden, I heard a loud disturbing voice outside the car. I raised my head up just in time to see Nicole, Alonso's ghetto ass baby mama, standing in his face, arguing. I knew I was the topic because I heard her tell him that he had some nerve bringing me to her house. This wasn't the first time she had got wrong with me, and I was getting sick of her ass.

I opened my door and threw one leg out. I stood, still with the other leg inside as I looked over the top of the car at them, standing in the yard, acting ratchet.

"Um, if you got something to say to me, here I am." I yelled out, acting just as ratchet. When I said that, it really got Nicole riled up.

"What? Bitch, I'll fuck your lil' young ass the fuck up!"

"Do it!"

Alonso look toward me and then his deep baritone voice barked, "Aye, girl, get yo' ass back in the damn car!"

"That's right, *girl*, get yo' ass back in the car, like *my nigga* said."

"Your nigga?" I'm not going to lie, that shit hit a damn nerve, but I wasn't going to give her ass the satisfaction of knowing that. "Bitch, if he was your nigga, you would be sitting yo' fat ass over here in this passenger seat, instead of me. Ya'll hoes can't stand the fact that this young ass girl took this nigga from ya'll." Being childish, I stuck my tongue out at her. "Bitch, you mad or nah?"

"Lonso, get yo' ass off me! That bitch talking a lot of shit right now." Alonso had to grab Nicole to keep her from coming out here. I know I had just called her fat, but she wasn't near fat. Homegirl had it going on.

Nicole was fucking beautiful, and she had a body to die for. Nonetheless, I wasn't about to compliment her on her looks or her body. Her thick ass was a lot bigger than my 5'6 petite self. So, every chance I got, I was sure to call her fat or ugly for the simple fact that I couldn't say shit else about her. She stayed dressing fly and dripped in diamonds, but just like she had it going on and dressed fly, I did the same.

In reality, neither of us could really say anything about the other's looks because we both were bad bitches. Only difference is, she had a house and car, and I didn't.

"La-La, I ain't telling yo' ass no more, get the fuck in the car! I'm not playing with you." I didn't have to be close up on Alonso to know he had lines formed on his forehead, because it happened every time he was upset, and right now, those lines signified he was that pissed at Nicole and my bullshit.

Sticking my tongue out at Nicole one last time, I got my ass right on in the car like *my man* said, and locked the door. Lets be real, I didn't want Nicole's ass to break free. There was no doubt in my mind that she would demolish my ass if she got her claws on me. No, I wasn't saying I couldn't fight, but girlfriend had a lot of hood in her, and she was about six or seven years older than me. She had been in the game for a while, so I knew she probably had hands for days. Still, that wouldn't make me bow down to her ass.

If she did break free of his hold, we would've been two fighting bitches.

One thing about me, Eliza Marie Brown, I didn't back down to anyone. I had only been in two fights, in middle school, and I'd won them both. So, I felt I'd give any bitch a run for their money, no matter how many years that had been, or how many years they had on me.

"Man, calm yo' ass down, Nicole. Like, dead ass." I had the window crack so I could hear what was said outside this car—which, I probably would've heard with the window still up, as loud as they were talking. My mind was still on her stating that Alonso, *my man*, was her nigga, and I was trying to see if it would be said why she felt that way. "I'm not about to let you fight my shawty. So you might as well just go on back in the house. You see these fucking kids and your neighbor out here looking and shit. Stop playing around before they call the fucking police."

"Fuck you, Alonso, and fuck these fucking neighbors! Let them call the police. I don't damn care!"

"Well, I do." When he said that, he whispered something into her ear. I didn't know what he said, but I could see her body relax right before he let her go. They had a stare off then she looked pass him and at his car. Desperately, I wanted to get out and ask him what in the fuck he'd just said to her, but I thought against it, knowing he would be getting in the car soon and I could ask him then. Plus, I knew had I said something, it would start that Chihuahua back up again.

She uttered something about me being lucky and told Alonso to never disrespect her like that again, by bringing me to her house, and then she turned around and walked inside, ushering their six year old son and her eight year old daughter, by another man, inside along with her.

When Alonso made it back to the car, I was pissed. Before he could even pull off, I was facing him and grilling him about what he'd said to calm her down. I asked, "What you whispered into her ear?"

"What?" Alonso cut his eyes at me as he pulled off, once again, like a bat out of hell. He was already a fast driver, and it worsened when he was pissed.

"What... Did... You... Say... to calm her down?" This time, I spoke slowly since it seemed he was having a hard time comprehending.

"Don't fucking talk to me like I'm slow, and I didn't really say shit. I just told the dumb ass girl that I had work on me and didn't need the pigs pulling up." My eyes narrowed as I gave him the side eye.

After what she'd said, I didn't want to believe him, but it did make sense. It didn't take a rocket scientist to know that he sold drugs, so I understood if he didn't want the police getting involved, and I damn sure didn't want those problems. Alonso was a big time drug dealer, and I wasn't trying to get locked up just from being in the car with him. However, being that his son had just gotten out the car with us, I knew he didn't have any drugs or anything illegal in the car. So that was the reason I gave him the side eye.

"Why did she say you was her nigga?" My stare was hard, just waiting to see how he would justify that shit. My heart was racing, hoping this man wasn't sleeping around on me. Had he been, it would've proven my mama and everybody else right. "What she meant by that?"

"I don't fucking know! Why you didn't ask her that when you was outside the car talking shit back to her?" Alonso cut his eyes at me as he stopped at the stoplight.

"I was trying but you made me get back inside, like you was scared she was going to tell something."

He laughed as if I'd just told the funniest joke of all time. "Tell something? Lil' Mama, she don't have shit to tell when it comes to me."

"Oh, so now I'm Lil' Mama again?" I was smiling on the inside but dared not to let my excitement show.

With a lick of his lips as his head shook, Alonso pulled off from the light that was now green. He mumbled, "What the fuck is you talking about, La-La? Since you wanna question me about everything, what that bullshit your mama was spitting when I called your phone?"

I sucked my teeth and turned my head to look out the passenger window. Here I was, praying he didn't hear her, and he had. I somewhat figure that was the cause of his little attitude, and I honestly didn't know why he let that get to him. That wasn't the first time he had heard her going off about us while we were on the phone. Hell, I still remembered when she had taken my phone and called him.

It was a few days after I had stayed out passed curfew. She'd gotten word that I had been kicking it with an older guy and came to my grandma's house and took my phone. She called him right then and there and went clean off.

Embarrassed would've been an understatement.

Alonso was so upset that he didn't talk to me for two weeks—which, he didn't have a way to call me if he wanted to, being that my mama had taken my phone. Yet and still, I called him every day from Zola and Chyna's phone, but he wouldn't accept my calls. Then one day, he was waiting for me after school and took me to get another phone. He told me that he wanted to be done with me because he understood where my mama was coming from, but he'd already grown feelings for me.

The feelings were mutual, because I'd falling in love with him the second my eyes had landed on him. So, imagine how sick I was when he was giving me the silent treatment.

"Oh, so, you don't hear me now? You just had a lot to say, but now you can't tell me what mom dukes was saying?" Alonso's voice brought me out my thoughts.

"She was saying the same bullshit." I turned to face him. "That you're too old for me, and she don't like us together."

"Nah... I heard something about her calling the cops."

I released a heavy sigh.

I knew Alonso hated the police, and that made me afraid that he would end things with me because of my mama's threat. Even so, to soothe his mind, I told him, "She's just talking shit, Lonso. You know how she is. Just continue to pick me up on the next block and—"

"And she won't call the police on my black ass, huh?" I got quiet. I knew he was tired of this, and so was I, but, what did he expect when he was dealing with a minor? I wanted us to be together and not have to sneak around, too, but until I was eighteen, this was how it was going to be.

2

Alonso Davis

On some real shit, I didn't even know how I allowed myself to fall for Lil' Mama as hard as I did. The last thing I wanted was for somebody to think I was some pedophile ass nigga that went around preying on little girls, because that wasn't the fucking case. When I first saw Eliza, she was at my brother's house. I'd gone there to pick up some money that nigga had for me.

Prince, my brother, wasn't my right hand man, or anything like that, but he worked for me. No, he wasn't no corner boy, either, but he picked up money and sometimes made drops. I didn't allow him to make too many drops because if that nigga got caught up, I wouldn't be able to live with myself, and I didn't want that bullshit on my conscience.

When I'd gone to his house that day, he was in the bedroom with Eliza's homegirl. Just like any other time, I used my key to let myself in. I was shocked to walk in, to Lil' Mama sitting on the couch. She had her feet thrown up while texting on her phone, eating chips, like she was at home. I mean, Lil' Mama was comfortable.

At the time, I thought she was my brother's girl. So, despite how sexy her ass was, I only asked her where my brother was so I could get what I had come for and leave.

It was then that I found out Prince was fucking with her friend. We got to talking, and shawty told me that she was eighteen. Had I known she was only seventeen, there's no way I would've even given her my number. My ass would've walked back out that door without so much of a fucking goodbye. Yeah, that was still young to my twenty-four-year-old ass, at the time, but she would've been legal.

The crazy part about it, I found out she was only seventeen through her moms. The day she called me, cursing my ass out for talking to her seventeen-year-old daughter, I felt like the dirtiest nigga in the gotdamn world. I cursed at myself because I should've known something was off. I used to try and get Eliza to come out during the middle of the night and she always had an excuse. Looking back, the truth was always in my face, but I was just too blind to see it.

Plus, I had other women. So I wasn't that fucked up over her not being able to come out and chill with me or being able to stay all night. After all, it was the beginning of us talking, so I wasn't tripping at all.

Even with her mama snapping on my ass, I didn't even snitch on Eliza by telling her mama that she had lied to a nigga about her age. I just sat there, letting mom dukes get everything off her chest. I didn't say shit, and when she ended the call in my face, I said to myself that, that was going to be the last time I would receive one of those calls about her daughter.

Yeah, I was planning on cutting Lil' Mama off.

Hell, I had even tried, but the shit wasn't as easy as I'd hoped it to be. I started missing the fuck out of her, and the crazy part about it, it wasn't even her pussy that a nigga was missing, because I had never stuck my dick in it, but it was *her company* that I missed most. Her being around. Her smile. The way she smelled. It was driving me insane, and unfortunately, I gave in to her.

We've been together for nine months, and the way I felt for Lil' Mama, I had never felt for anyone else, not even Nicole, and she was the mother of my child.

"Bae?" Eliza said when we were inside my condo. I had a house over in the hood that I stayed at from time to time, but my condo in the downtown part of Atlanta was something special to me. I didn't let too many mothafuckas over here, because I wanted something I could lay back in and not have to worry about being bothered. And the thing I loved about it most was, you had to have a code to even get through the gate and into the building.

Although this was where Eliza and I usually chilled when we were together, she still didn't have that code. She was still young, so who's to say we'll have that forever kind of love.

"What's up?" I walked back into the living room and flopped down on the couch where she was. As I was bringing my beer to my mouth, she crawled on top of me, straddling me in a riding position. Placing the palm of her hands on my chest, she started rubbing in a circular motion, as she looked me directly in the eyes.

"I don't want you to leave me. Like, I know this is tiring for you, because it is for me…" Leaning down, she planted her lips on mine, giving me a peck before positioning herself back like she was. "But, think about it, I'll be eighteen in a couple of months, and I know things will get better for us. I can be all yours, and it ain't a damn thing my mama can say about it."

She tried to come in for another kiss, but I took my beer to the head to prevent her from kissing me. There was sadness in her eyes as we continued staring at one another while I drunk my beer. It wasn't until I brought it from my mouth that I asked, "Do you really think your mom is going to be okay with us being together, all because you're eighteen, La-La? She don't give a fuck about that. This shit is going to forever go on with her talking shit because she don't like my ass, and probably never will."

"And?" Eliza looked at me like I was crazy. "I'll be eighteen, Lonso. It ain't shit she can say about that. What can she do, put me out? So, what… Let her do it."

"Fuck you mean, let her do it?" This time, it was me that looked at her like she was crazy. I loved Lil' Mama and everything, but I thought she was going overboard by saying that, because had she got put out, the first person she would call was me. At the end of the day, she was still a lot younger than me, and I didn't even know if I was ready to be shacking up with anyone.

The hurt that washed over Eliza's face when I said that stabbed at my heart. I knew what was running through her mind, and I didn't for one second want her to think I didn't love her or want to be with her. I did, but the living together part was a bit too much right now.

Just as I suspected, she thought that, and it showed when she tried climbing off my lap. I wrapped my free hand around her and leaned over to sit the beer on the coffee table. "Man, you know I didn't mean it like that."

She tried getting off me again as she told me, "Nah, it's all good. I wasn't trying to move in here if that's what you were thinking. I was just saying. If she wanna put me out because I wanna be with you, then let her do it. I guess you was the one that read too much into it."

She was lying, but I played along.

"I know what you meant, and I was saying, you don't need to be like that. You know, acting like you don't care and shit. You know you can always crash at my place." I prayed I wasn't putting my foot in my damn mouth by saying that shit.

"Nah, I'm good. Trust me, I got other options." This time, she pushed my hand away from her body and quickly hopped up before I could grab her, knowing she had just pissed me off by spitting that. I hopped up and was all over her ass.

"Fuck you mean you got other options?" I grabbed her by the arm, spinning her around to face me.

"Just what I said, and how in the hell you going to get mad because I said that when you—"

"Eliza, don't get fucked up in here!" I cut her ass off because I didn't want to hear that shit. My eyebrows raised and I could feel the wrinkles in my forehead forming. I hated how jealous she made my ass feel. "Who your other fucking option? Better be your damn grandparents."

Eliza pressed her lips together, rolled her eyes and then said, "Wouldn't you like to know, but it wouldn't be here."

Grabbing her other arm, I threw her ass against the wall so fast, causing a scream to escape her mouth. When she saw I had a look that said I wasn't playing with her ass, she busted out laughing.

"I was just playing with you, Lonso. Now let me go." I didn't because I didn't believe she was playing. Well, a part of me did, but the other part thought she was only saying that to get me to let her go and that part caused me to squeeze her arms tighter. "Bae, stop before you put a bruise on me. I told you I was only playing. Dang."

"You been fucking around, Shawty?"

"What? No, Lonso! Why would you ask me something like that?" I could tell her little feelings were hurt, but shit, I wanted to know since she felt the need to play around and shit. When I didn't say anything back, she then shouted. "I'm still a damn virgin, fool. Do you wanna stick your dick in me and see for yourself?"

She looked pissed, and I knew she was telling the truth. Her eyes had even watered up, and it made me feel bad for asking that dumb ass question. So bad that I let her go and then took a step back. Yet, I continued eyeing her hard.

I said, "Man, why the fuck you play so damn much?"

"No, you playing." She rolled those damn eyes of hers. "Asking a question that you already know the answer to. You know I'm not out here fucking around, but yet, you wanna ask that stupid question." The scowl that Eliza once wore on her face softened as she walked up on me and wrapped her arms around my neck. Standing on her tiptoes, she started placing soft kisses on my lips. Immediately, my dick stiffened, just from her touch alone. "You know I'm saving myself for you. You know you're the only man I want... In more ways than one."

I knew Eliza was saving herself for me. It was just... my fucking bruised ego that caused me to ask her that question.

"I know... My bad about that." I apologized. "But you can't be saying no shit like that, girl. You gon' have me out here fucking niggas up." As my sentenced ended, I lifted her body into my arms, causing her to automatically lock her legs around my waist as I buried my head in the crook of her neck. I walked us over to the couch and took a seat, never missing a beat with sucking and kissing all over her neck.

"Lonso, don't put no damn hickey on my neck."

"I'm not. Damn, chill." *See?* Little shit like that reminded me how fucked up this situation truly was. It reminded me that I needed to let this damn young ass girl go, and find me a real woman, but that shit was easier said than done. Eliza was like a forbidden fruit, and I just couldn't get enough of her. We all wanted what we couldn't have or shouldn't have. That's how I felt when it came to her.

On some real shit, I never thought I would feel this way about a woman this much younger than me, but here I was, head over fucking heels for this damn girl.

"I wanna do it, Alonso." Eliza announced through a moan as I sat on the couch with her straddling me. She was now kissing all over my neck while rotating her hips against my midsection. My dick was hard as hell, and she was trying to feel every inch of it.

Through a groan as I leaned my head back and closed my eyes, I told her, "Come on now, Lil' Mama, you know we can't do that."

"Why?" At this point, she started tugging with my belt buckle. "I wanna feel you inside of me, and not just my mouth. I want all of you, Alonso Davis." Easing back, she released my dick from my pants and started stroking it while now looking me in the eyes. Her eyes were filled with lust as she bit down on her bottom lip in a way that was driving me crazy. When she did little shit like that, it made it hard to tell her no. "You said this was my dick, right?"

"It is yours. You know that."

"Well, why can't I have it inside of me? Why won't you make love to me? Just once, and I won't ask no more." She leaned over and kissed me passionately, and when the kiss ended, her forehead pressed against mine as she mumbled against my lips, "Baby, please... Just take my virginity."

I had to get her off me. Had she continued stroking my dick and grinding her pussy on my shit, I was going to be forced to do some shit I didn't want to do, and that was take her virginity right now.

"I can't, bae." I brought my hand up to caress the back of her neck.

"We already don't suppose to be together. Your mom wanna call the cops on me and shit... I can't fuck you."

"But what's the difference with us doing other stuff? You let me go down on you, and you go down on me." I didn't say anything because she had a point. "Plus, my mama already thinks I'm having sex with you. So, we might as well go ahead and do it."

"Just because she think that doesn't mean we can fuck." I chuckled as she rolled her eyes and sucked her teeth. "Yo' damn eyes going to get stuck with the way you keep rolling them mothafuckas. And what the hell you pouting for, La-La?"

"Because everybody else is having sex, but my own damn boyfriend won't even have sex with me."

I frowned and looked at her like she was crazy for saying that stupid ass shit. "So you tryna get fucked because your best bitches forever is fucking? You wanna be like those hoes?"

I knew that was the name of their little group message and shit. And when I called her little friends hoes, that's what the fuck I meant. I didn't personally know them, but I saw right through their asses. They were fucking for their next come up, and my brother and home-boy, Clarence, were their new victims.

"Why do they have to be hoes, Alonso?"

"Because they are." I was saying as she got off my lap. "And they're bad influence on you, too."

"So what, you my daddy now? You wanna tell me who I can and can't hang around?"

"I'm not tryna tell you who you can and can't hang around, and I'm damn sure not trying to play the role of your pops." I stood and stuffed my dick back into my pants then leaned down to grab my keys off the end table. "I'm just speaking the truth. Look at you, wanting to have sex because those hoes are. That's one of the reasons I won't fuck you, because you're acting thirsty for a dick just like them."

Eliza's mouth damn near hit the floor when I spoke the truth. I didn't care how offended she was, I was speaking straight facts.

"I cannot believe you just said that, Alonso. It's one thing to keep talking out the side of your neck about my friends, but to say I'm thirsty for a dick was downright fucked up." She snatched her purse off the couch and threw it on her shoulders. I guess she was feeling the same as me right now—that this little time we were supposed to be spending together was over. She walked to the door with me following. Placing her hand on the knob, she jerked her body around to face me and said, "Oh, and FYI, I'm not thirsty for a dick, I'm thirsty for my man's dick, and his only."

With that, she opened the door and walked off, leaving me to shake my head and do the same.

3

Eliza Brown

*A*lonso had pissed me off so bad that the whole ride to drop me off, I didn't say shit to him. He was out of pocket for the stuff he was saying back at his place, and he knew that. I hated when he would bad mouth my friends, and he always made it a point to say something slick about them. I was so freakin' mad that I didn't even ask where he was going after I got out his car. It was so crazy that the part that angered me the most was the fact that he wouldn't have sex with me, and I felt I had every right to be mad.

I wanted to feel Alonso, but he just wouldn't let me feel him the way I wanted to, and it pissed me off.

When he pulled up to the corner of my street to drop me off, I got out and didn't even say bye, and neither did he. Yet, he continued sitting there, watching me walk home like he always did.

I couldn't even front like my boo wasn't a sweetheart, because he truly was.

"La-La, is that you?" My mama yelled from her bedroom. I rolled my eyes, thinking who else could it have been.

"Yeah, it's me." I headed straight into the kitchen, washed my hands and started fixing me something to eat. When I left, my mama was cooking a pot roast, and I couldn't wait to get some because a sister was starving like Marvin.

"Did you wash your hands before going in my food?"

"Ma, don't I always wash my hands?" My back was to her while I rolled my eyes like she could see them.

"That nigga must didn't feed you?" I didn't say anything back to her for the simple fact that I knew she was trying to start an argument. "And I'm glad you came home early, so you can help me go out there and clean that shed. I wanna make me a garden, and I'ma need somewhere to store my stuff that I'm going to need to start it. Okay?"

I swear, this lady was so bipolar that it was ridiculous. One minute she was cursing me out, and the next she was talking to me like she actually had some sense.

"Okay. We can start on it when I finish eating. It's not going to take me long."

She nodded her head and walked off, puffing on her cigarette.

Twenty minutes later, my mom and I were out back, cleaning the shed. It was so crazy because both of us were scared, praying we didn't run up on any possums, snakes or anything else that would possibly harm us. It took us three freakin' hours to clean that shed, and we still had more to do after I got home from school tomorrow. My mama made sure to tell me that I better had been home by the time she got off work at 6pm., and I was sure to let her know that I would be, because I didn't have anywhere else to go.

I knew she wanted to grill my ass because it was rare for me to be home when she got off work.

Inside the house, I showered and locked myself inside my bedroom. I was on my way to sleep until Chyna called. My girls shared a ringtone, so I knew it was either her or Zola calling me.

"What's up, Chy?" I answered after seeing her name on the screen.

"What in the hell is wrong with you and yo' nigga? Is he still on his fucking period?" She yelled into the phone, her Spanish accent was in full effect. Chyna was mixed with Mexican and Black, and when she talked fast or was upset, her Spanish accent would be thick. It was cute, but at the same time, you couldn't understand shit she was saying. Hell, you would be lucky if she didn't just start speaking Spanish all together, never minding you didn't speak that language.

"What?" I frowned, hating when she would call herself talking bad about my boo—which, she didn't care who it was, Chyna didn't bite her tongue for anyone. "What make you think something is wrong with us?"

"Because I'm at Clarence house and he was just here."

"And?"

"And I asked him where you was, and let's just say, if looks could kill, my ass would've been fucking dead. Then he going to say he didn't fucking know, like he doesn't be keeping tabs on your ass."

I sucked my teeth and shook my head as I sank deeper into my bed. I hated when Alonso and I were at odds because he would completely shut me out and have me walking around like I'd lost my best friend.

"Girl, I'll tell you about it tomorrow at school. You still at Clare's house?" I called her boyfriend by his nickname that everybody called him, except Chyna and his mama. When she told me that she was there and was staying all night over there, I asked her, "So, you not going to school tomorrow? Chy, we'll be graduating soon, and you don't need to be—"

"Girl, I'm not missing no days. My black ass will be there bright and early. I've come too far to let a dick stop me from graduating." I laughed when she said that. While Chyna and I were on our last year of high school, Zola had graduated the year before. So now, she had all the time in the world to spend with Prince—which, school didn't stop Chyna from spending her nights with Clarence. Unlike my mama, their parents didn't give a damn what they did, or who they did it with, and it had been that way long before they turned eighteen. "Anyways, Clarence is dropping me off in the morning. You want us to come pick you up?"

"Nah, I'll go ahead and ride the bus. Ya'll asses be trying to do too much, wanting to stop and get food when we're already late and shit.

The last thing I need is for my mama to think I'm late for school because of Alonso. You know she already don't like him."

"Girl, tell Erika to take a chill pill. Damn. I swear, she's worse than the feds."

"I know, right. We got into a whole ass argument when I got ready to leave with him earlier today."

"I bet you can't wait to turn eighteen. I bet you moving in with him and everything, because you know Erika still ain't going to let that fool come over there." Chyna laughed before she started coughing. I knew she was smoking weed because that was all she did. Out of the three of us, Chyna was the fun friend. The one everybody wanted to hang around or be like. She wasn't only beautiful with an exotic appearance, but the girl knew how to have fun, too.

She was the life of the party, hands down.

"I don't know about all that." My voice was nonchalant as I thought back on earlier when I was at Alonso's place, how he tried to play me. The nigga pretty much kicked it like he didn't want me to move in with him, and then when I got mad, he tried to change it up like that wasn't what he meant.

Who the fuck does that?

"What you mean? Girl, that man is just on his period right now. When he get off, ya'll will be right back acting all in love and shit. You know Alonso ain't trying to fuck up with ya'll have. He's too scared that someone else will get that pussy before him."

See? See what I meant? This damn girl was so damn blunt that it wasn't funny. She didn't have no filter, whatsoever.

"Well, damn, thanks. You didn't say he wasn't trying to fuck up because he loves me, but because he was scared someone else would take my virginity. Wow. You really know how to make a girl feel good about herself, Chyna."

"Oh, hush, Mamacita. You know what I meant. But look, I'll call you in the morning. I hear Clarence coming in and I don't need his ass trying to be nosey and shit." With a laugh, I told her okay and we ended the call. All I could do was shake my head at her antics. I knew she didn't mean any harm in what she had just said, but it did make me think.

Alonso was quick to throw our age difference in my face, but he wouldn't leave me alone. He made it clear that he would fuck up any nigga that tried to get next to me, and now with Chyna saying that, it made me wonder if that was true. I refused to sit around thinking he really loved me when all the while, he was just waiting until I was eighteen to take my virginity and drop me like a bad habit.

I had to laugh at my own antics—at all the bullshit that was running through my mind.

Alonso did love me. I knew it. I felt it deep in my soul. I could see it in his eyes when he looked at me. Hear it in his voice when he spoke to me. He loved me, and my boo wasn't like these other guys. He was different, and I wasn't about to let what Chyna said get to me or have me thinking anything different about him or questioning his love for me. No matter the age difference, Alonso and I were destined to be together, and I couldn't wait to prove everyone wrong about our love.

THE NEXT MORNING, CHYNA CALLED ME BRIGHT AND EARLY TO LET ME know that she was pushing one of Clarence's whips to school. She said he was complaining about having to wake up and take her, so he told her to take one. This was the first time he had ever let her drive one of his cars, so my girl was on cloud nine right now.

"Bitch, you know a nigga sprung off your good stuff when he let you hold one of the whips," I boosted her ego as I hopped into the passenger seat. "Let me find out you been over there laying it down and shit."

Chyna stuck her tongue out and started popping her coochie in her seat, causing me to laugh and shake my head.

"I can't wait to call and tell Zola this. This shit is official now, and you know these hoes is about to start hating once they see you pushing his car."

"And I'm ready for one of his hoes to try and run up. I'm knocking the first bitch the fuck out that try me." We laughed. "We're gonna have to work on getting you your Ls so we all can be pushing these niggas whips, making all these hoes jealous and shit." My girl was so amped up at the thought of that. I mean, it did sound nice. Even I had to admit that.

"I know right," was my only reply. Driving had never been a priority to me. The only places I went other than to the store, was to Zola and Chyna's house, and if I had to go to the store or anywhere else, my mom would take me, or I would walk if it weren't too far. Hell, sometime Zola would get one of her parents' cars to drive us around. So, yeah... driving had never been a priority for me.

As we got closer to our school, Chyna reached over and turned the radio up to the max. One couldn't tell us that we weren't the shit right now. We were in high school pushing a damn Audi... Yeah, hoes were definitely about to start hating.

"Okay, I see you, Chyna," said a guy named Tyrell. He was hopping out is car when we pulled up and parked beside him. Once upon a time, Tyrell was cool, but that was before he started feeling himself. He was a jackass at heart now, and thought he was just god's gift to women.

The type that thought he could have his cake and eat it, too. I guess because he was used to getting his way—used to the females letting him play them right in their faces. Tyrell was the star basketball player, and all the girls wanted him. Even I had to admit, the brother had it going on.

"So, what's up, La-La? Why you ain't pushing yo' man's whip?" he asked me.

"Why push his when I can ride with my homegirl?" He didn't need to know that I didn't have no license. "And why you worried about me? You need to be worried about Aria. I heard ya'll was boo'd up at the mall Saturday."

Tyrell's eyes went dead to Chyna. She threw her hands in the air so fast and shook her head. Laughing, she told him, "Don't look at me. I didn't talk to her about shit I saw at the mall."

"Right." I co-signed. "She didn't tell me anything."

"Ooooh." A wide grew on his face as his head bobbed up and down. With a quick lick of his lips, he said, "I figured Zola was going to go back and run her mouth, but it don't matter..." He jumped his shoulders. "It is what it is. I mean, it ain't like you tryna give a nigga a chance."

"You right. You blew your chance. Remember? I gave you my number, and a week of us talking, I show up at the skating rink and you hugged up with another bitch."

Tyrell licked his lips as he quickly turned his head as an ounce of embarrassment washed over his face. He turned back to look at me and then said, "Man, chill out with that. Why you bringing up old shit? I didn't even know you were going to be there. You said you was staying at home."

"So that makes it right for you to try and play me like that?"

Chyna chimed in, adding her two cents, "Exactly. I swear, ya'll niggas ain't shit."

"Chyna, shut the hell up. You ain't shit, either." When he said that, Chyna tried to kick him. And no, it wasn't because she was trying to hush him or anything like that, because I knew all about her getting drunk last year and letting Tyrell and two of his homeboys run a train on her.

When Zola told me that, I couldn't believe it. Not because Chyna had slept with him, but because she let all three of those niggas fuck her at the same time. Only hoes did stuff like that, and my girl wasn't one—at least I didn't think she was.

If you ask me, those fools took advantage of her that night.

She was drunk and wasn't in her right mind. Furthermore, she didn't have Zola or me there to let her know when she'd reached her limit. Chyna was so embarrassed that she didn't come to school for a week after that, and she kept apologizing to me. But I was sure to let her know that whatever happened with her and Tyrell that night wasn't going to come between our friendship. Talking on the phone for a week damn sure didn't make him my man.

"You a jackass, Tyrell!" Chyna yelled at his back due to him taking off running after saying that foul shit to her. "I swear, I hate that boy, and I know he was talking about the night I wished wouldn't have ever happened. I should've never gone to that party."

"Yeah, he is childish for that. Cute, but childish as fuck."

"On some real shit, I don't even think he's all that cute. His ways make him ugly as hell."

"Yeah, he's cocky as hell, but that shit don't take away from his looks, Chy. I would never let him know that, though."

"I guess..." Chyna rolled her eyes as we were approaching the building to go inside the school. We still had about five minutes before the bell rung, and she wanted to know what was going on with Alonso and me. She asked, "So, what happened with you and your man?"

I told her everything that happened—from the moment I got in the car with him to the moment I got out up the street from my house, leaving out what he had to say about her and Zola. I had to talk fast and still had a minute or two to spare before the bell rung for us to get to homeroom.

"Damn, Mamacita. And what in the hell that bitch mean, *her nigga*? Is he still fucking her?"

"Girl, I do not know. I mean, he's not fucking me. So he has to be sleeping with someone, right?"

"Not necessarily. I mean, just ask him." I shook my head, never mentioning that I had asked him that several times before, and his answer was always no. A part of me felt like a fool for even believing him. "I'm not trying to tell you to do something that you're not ready to do, but if you feel he is sleeping around, maybe you need to step your game up."

"But that's just it. I *been* trying to step my game up." I let out a frustrated chuckle, emphasizing the word been. "Us going down on each other is only going to last for so long. Like, I feel I'm ready to consummate our relationship. We've been together for almost a year and I know we love each other. I wanna be with him forever. I might be young, but I know he's the man I wanna spend the rest of my life with."

As my sentence was ending the first bell rung, meaning we needed to be ending this conversation.

"Well, you'll be eighteen soon. Maybe that's what he's waiting on, but let me get to class. I'm not trying to be late." With that, she walked off before I could get anything else out, leaving me to turn around and head to my class as well.

While walking there, I took my phone out my back pocket to send Alonso a text. All I said was, *I love you and I hope you have a good day.* Being that we'd had that little argument, I really wasn't expecting for him to text back, but he did.

Alonso: I'll be out front to get you when you get out. I miss you.

Eliza: I miss you, too, and okay.

I didn't bother telling him through a text, but the minute I got in his car, it was a must I told him that I needed to be home before six. Whether he got mad or not, I couldn't leave my mama hanging like that—not when I promised to help her. I might've been a rebellious child at times, but I wasn't going to do that. Plus, I would never hear the end of it if I did.

4

Chyna Wilson

My mind had been on everything but my schoolwork all day, and I had Tyrell's dumb ass to think for that. He just had to bring up old shit, and how he figured I wasn't shit because of a slip up was beyond me. But, I will say this, I felt that same way the day after it all happened. I couldn't even face Eliza because at one time, she liked Tyrell, and for me to sex not only him but his friends as well was embarrassing and downright disgusting. Hell, I couldn't face anyone, especially after learning some idiot had recorded it for the world to see.

It took me weeks to get to the point where I didn't want to just kill myself. Millions of mothafuckas had seen me naked—had seen me sucking dicks and shit. When Zola showed me the video and said someone had sent it to her, I felt like the dirtiest bitch on the planet, and no amount of times I washed my body, I couldn't get clean. And don't let me get started on Eliza. It took me a long time to face her, but she was sure to let me know that she and Tyrell weren't a couple and never would be, and even told me that she knew what had gone down that night was a mistake—which, it was.

Eliza and Zola knew me better than I knew myself, and they knew I would never sleep with more than one guy at a time. I was drunk, way passed my limit, and those niggas knew that. No, I wasn't saying they raped me, or anything like that, but they damn sure took advantage of the situation. And for Tyrell to throw it in my face was wrong on so many levels.

Eliza told me at lunch that Alonso was picking her up today, so I didn't even make it to my last period. I wasn't feeling it today, and I was surprised I even lasted that long.

"Hey, I'm on my way."

"What? What you mean you on your way? What time is it?" Clarence voice was muzzily, letting me know that he was either still asleep or had just wakened up not too long ago. Clarence weren't a morning person, and anytime I would stay at his house on a school night, I would damn near have to beat his ass in order for him to get up and drive me to school. This morning he said fuck it, though. Shit, I halfway wanted to say it my damn self. We didn't go to sleep until five a.m., and my ass was beyond tired.

"It's almost one, and you need to get up so you can take me home."

"Home? Fuck you going home for?"

I wasn't really ready to go, but anytime I was over there for more than two days, I would fake like I wanted to, just so I wouldn't wear out my welcome. And, I liked to hear my nigga beg me to stay, knowing all along he didn't have to beg for shit when it came to me.

"Because I need to get me some clothes. I need to go to the store to get some feminine stuff and all that."

"Okay, you can go later on."

"Ugh. Clarence, you always trying to do stuff on your term. Why I can't ever do shit when I want to? What are you doing now? Why can't you take me home when I get there?" I waited for him to reply, and when he didn't, I said, "Hello?"

I thought he had gone back to sleep on me, but his lazy ass had hung up in my face. I hit his name to call him back, but before it started ringing, I ended the call. I wasn't too far from his house, so I just decided to wait until I got there to start an argument.

Clarence stayed in the hood. Like, it was so fucking hood where he lived that I didn't see how he had all this nice shit in his house, and nobody ever broke in or tried to steal one of his nice cars. It wasn't like he had a garage to park them in. It was crazy, but I guess when you had the street credibility as him, everybody knew not to fuck with you.

"Why did you hang up on me?" I yelled when I walked inside, using the door key that was on the key ring to let myself in. I knew it was that key because I had to lock the top lock with it this morning. "You so damn rude, Clarence."

"Man, don't come in here with all that fucking yelling!" When I made it to the back of the house to his bedroom, he was coming out the bathroom, washing his face. "And I hung up because I wasn't trying to hear that shit. You ain't about to go home no time soon. So, I don't even know why you called with that bullshit."

"I am about to go home. I been here for four days. My mama wanna see me. You just seen your mama yesterday, didn't you?" When he turned around and just walked back into the bathroom, I yelled, "Exactly! You seen yours and I'm going to see mine. Point fucking blank! Period, pooh."

My back was to him when I said that. I was walking over to the bed to lay across it when he grabbed me from behind. He had one arm wrapped around my body and the other one around my neck, playing like he was about to choke me out.

I screamed as he pushed my upper body down on the bed.

"Nah, don't scream now. Keep talking that big boy shit."

By now, I was laughing because I knew exactly what he was trying to do, get him some.

"Move! I'm not even playing with you. I need to pack the lil' shit I have over here so you can take me home."

Smack.

He smacked my butt and told me to shut up, causing a purr to escape my mouth. "Oooh, Papi, I like it rough."

"Yeah, I know you do, and I'm about to give it to you rough."

By now, this man was pulling my jeans down. I was no longer trying to put up a fight or act like I didn't want this, because I did.

Probably just as bad as he did right about now. When he ripped off the thong I had on, I cursed him out. Fooling around with his ass, I wasn't going to have any underwear to wear. He always did this crazy shit, and then when I fussed, he'd say, *you don't need them on anyways.* I didn't know what Clarence had against panties, but he never wanted me to wear any—talking about some easy access.

Easy access my ass.

"Oh, no. You better get one of those condoms from in the damn drawer, Clarence. I'm not playing with you." I wasn't trying to have nobody's damn child.

"Man, just let me do it once without it. I'll pull out."

"No!" I tried to get up, but he pushed me back down. When he did it for the second time, I felt myself getting pissed. "Clarence, stop. I'm not even playing."

"Man, why you tripping? You let me do it before without one."

"And what happened with that? We got a scare."

He froze, I guess thinking back three months ago when he tried to run that same lie to me—that he would pull out. He didn't and the next month my damn cycle was late, and I was going crazy, thinking I was pregnant. I wasn't falling for it this time around, and he knew that, too. That's why he stepped back and walked his ass the short distance to the nightstand to retrieve a condom. When he ripped it with his teeth, I smiled through pressed lips.

"That's what I thought!" I said.

"What?" I giggled and threw my face against the mattress as his eyebrow raised when he looked at me. As he stepped behind me, he grabbed my waist and yanked my body up to him with force. "You on one today, shawty, but I got something for that ass."

Clarence rammed his dick in my opening as the words left his mouth, causing me to squeal and fall right back down, flat on my stomach. I yelled, "Hold on now, mothafucka..."

"Nawl... Fuck, no! You like it rough, remember."

I turned around to face him, but he pushed my head back down to the mattress. Even so, I still mumbled, "But you can't be ramming—"

"I can't be what?" He did the stupid shit again, but this time, I clutched the covers and arched my back more. "That's right, arch that fucking back. You know you like this shit, so stop frontin'."

And he was right. I liked it. In fact, I fucking loved it, but even that didn't mean it didn't hurt when it hit the bottom of my stomach. It was a good pleasurable, pain, though. One that I should've been used to since we had been fucking for almost a year, and I had been having the best time of my life since I met him.

Ironically, Zola introduce me to him a week after Eliza had met Alonso. She was talking about some triple date shit, and we hadn't been on one with these niggas yet. Hell, it was barely a time that all six of us were at the same place together.

"Shit... Damn, baby." I was grinding my ass against his dick as he gave me slow, long strokes. One of his hands was pressing my lower back down, while the other one had a hand full of my hair. See, shit like that had a bitch falling harder and harder for his ass. "Baby, you about to make me cum..."

Leaning down, he started kissing on my back, causing me to arch it more, like I was about to break my spine.

"Clarence... Ssss... Clarence... I'm about to cum, baby." Just the feel of his lips on my back caused me to cream all over his condom-covered dick. Clarence continued stroking me nice and slow before he stood up, took a step back and then told me to take off all my close. He said he wanted me ass naked, and then instructed me to lay on my back. I did everything he said and then spread my legs like an eagle.

Clarence didn't waste no time positioning himself in between my thick thighs. As he leaned down to plant his lips on mine, I felt the head of his hard dick poking at my opening. I wrapped my arms around his neck as my legs went around his body. With the heel of my feet, I tried pulling his midsection further into mine. It wasn't long before he got the picture and pushed his dick into my pussy, making me hiss like a snake.

The man was really making love to my body and soul right now, in the middle of the day. I was under the impression that this was about to be a quickie—a quick little fuck session to shut me the hell up. However, my Papi had something else in mind, and I wasn't going to act like I wasn't enjoying it.

"Damn, this pussy good as fuck, girl," Clarence murmured against my mouth. When he pulled back from the kiss, he just stared at me, dead in the eyes. I smiled as his head shook before he buried it in the crook of my neck. His breathing had thickened, and I could feel that he'd added a little more force to his thrusts.

I pulled his body into mind as my legs and arms squeezed tighter around him. His lips parted and I could feel his teeth as they bit down on my neck. He sucked hard, and I knew a passion mark would be there by the time this session was over, but I didn't care. It wouldn't have been the first, and I knew for sure it wasn't going to be the last.

Clarence sucked harder. His paced sped up. He grunted and released my neck long enough to tell me that I had the best pussy in the world. He then found a fresh spot and started back sucking on my neck just as hard as he was before. I closed my eyes and enjoyed the bliss he had me in. My moans grew in his ear as I threw my pussy back to him, feeling an orgasm forming.

"Shit... Shit... Fuck." He cursed, and I could feel the sheets gathering underneath me. He was clutching them. I knew he was about to nut, so I started throwing my pussy back to him and talking in Spanish, something I knew for sure would bring that nut right on out of him.

Just like I knew my trick would work, Clarence was nutting in seconds, and it was at the same time I was releasing a mind-blowing orgasm.

"Damn, girl..." Clarence said as he stood to his feet after his breathing was under controlled. He looked down at his limp dick and started pulling the condom off. When he had it off, the fool had the nerve to hold it up, examining his work. "Look at this shit. I guess it is a good thing you made me wrap up. Yo' ass would've damn sure gotten pregnant off this shit. You see it?"

I rolled off the foot of the bed.

"Yeah, and I'm trying not to. Go throw that nasty shit in the trash, dude." While saying that, I was walking pass him to go to the bathroom. He smacked my butt as I walked by.

"Hold up before you use it. Let me flush this. I don't throw my rubbers in the trash. My mama taught me that a long time ago. Next thing I know I'll have about nine kids running around here."

"Nah, it'll only be eight, because you don't have to worry about me trying to trap yo' ass. But me on the other hand, I got something to be worried about because you always trying to trap me." I said that because he was forever trying to run up in me raw.

"Yo' ass wish I was trying to trap you." I didn't say anything in return when he yelled that out from his bedroom. Inside the bathroom, I handled my business and turned on the shower. "Aye, let me get in with you, Lonso pulling up in a minute."

We showered and had us a quick little fuck session before getting out. Clarence promised to take me home later on tonight, but he made it clear that he was only taking me to get some clothes. I said okay, but if he took me home, I was going to stay there for a few days. I knew my mama didn't care, but I still didn't want her thinking I had moved out. See, as long as I didn't let anything interfere with me graduating, my mama could care less what I did.

I was the oldest out of the six kids she had, and she felt once I had turned sixteen, I was old enough to make my own decisions. After all, it was one less mouth she had to feed. My father didn't care one way or the other, either, because when he wasn't working, he was feeding his body with drugs. So, nothing really mattered to him.

While Clarence went outside to kick it with the folks on his block, I smoked a half of blunt and took me a nap on the couch. I didn't know how long I had been asleep, but Eliza shaking me and calling my name awakened me.

"Hum?"

"Damn, girl. Are you okay? I been trying to wake you up for almost five minutes," she said.

I wiped the slob from the corner of my mouth and slowly sat up. That sex session and blunt had put me on my ass. "Yeah. I was just tired. What's up?" I looked around. "Where's Clarence?"

"He out there with Lonso. You know I wasn't trying to stand around in their face, and why you leave early? I was looking for you when I got outside."

"Because I wasn't feeling like that shit today. I just missed last period, though."

She nodded her head. We talked for a little while longer before Clarence and Lonso walked in. I took one look at Lonso and shook my head at him.

"I don't know why you was acting all funky yesterday when I asked you where she was, talking about some you didn't know." I rolled my eyes at him.

"Because I didn't know. If you wanted to know then you should've called her yourself," his smartass mouth said, and I wasn't backing down to his ass.

"But you did know."

"Chyna, will you leave my man alone. Damn."

I rolled my eyes when Eliza said that as I waved her off. "Girl, you know you don't want nobody saying nothing about his ass."

"And that's how it's supposed to be," Alonso said instead of her. I just rolled my eyes and said, whatever, as Eliza turned to look at him, asking if he was ready to go.

At first, I thought she wanted to leave because of me, but that went out the window when she told him "Remember what I told you."

"Yeah." Alonso ran his hand down his face and then motioned like he was about to open the front door, but Clarence big mouth stopped him.

"Aye, Chyna can drop her off on her way to get some clothes from her house. That'll get you from having to come all the way back over here."

Alonso said, "Oh hell yeah. Bet."

Don't get it twisted, I didn't have a problem dropping my girl off, but I really wasn't planning on driving Clarence car home because my intention was to not come back tonight. Eliza and I were looking confused, wondering when this were a part of the plan. Yet, it was me that spoke up, "Hold on. I was staying at home for the night. You don't like getting up in the mornings."

"Didn't you drive my car today? You can drive the shit tomorrow."

"How about I just stay home and bring the car back after school tomo—"

He cut me off and said a hard, *hell nawl*, causing everybody to laugh. "Yo' crack headed ass daddy ain't about to sell my shit."

My jaw dropped when he said that, as I looked over at Eliza to see her wearing the same facial expression. Her nigga was laughing his ass off, pissing me off more. "I don't see shit funny, and you asshole —" I turned back around and glared at Clarence. "You was wrong as hell for that."

When he saw that I was not only mad, but also hurt by what he'd said, he pulled me into his arms and kissed my lips. In my ear, he whispered, "I'm sorry, boo. You know I was just fucking around."

"Whatever." I rolled my eyes as I pushed myself out his arms and walked to the back of the house to get my things to leave. Sure, we joked around about my dad's drug habit, and even about his alcoholic ass mama, but never once had we done the shit in front of other people.

Now that I saw how he wanted to play, it was all fair games and nobody's ass was off limits.

5

Alonso Davis

"Man, why you say that shit about that girl's daddy?" I asked, still laughing, when Chyna walked to the back of the house. I was laughing so hard because we personally knew her pops. He had been buying dope from us long before Clarence started fucking with Chyna. To be honest, we were surprised that was even her pops when we found out.

Clarence and me, both, thought the nigga was capping when he stepped to Clarence and brought up Chyna, saying she was his daughter and he didn't want it getting back to her that he knew us. I took that as he was scared one of us was going to tell his baby girl how he be out begging for drugs and shit when he didn't have the money to get it.

"Lonso, that's not funny," Eliza slapped me on the arm as she mugged me. Still smiling, but not laughing as hard, I grabbed her and pulled her into my arms. "Your ignorant friend hurt my girl's feelings."

Clarence was now in the back room with Chyna, I guess trying to make up for what he'd said.

"It might not have been to ya'll, but that shit was dead ass funny to me." Leaning down, I kissed her lips before taking the bottom one into my mouth and biting down on it. When she tried to pull back, I bit down harder. When I finally let go, she hit me and laughed. "So, what you about to go home and do? I know you said you about to help your moms do something, but what?"

"Finish cleaning our shed. We started yesterday and wanna go ahead and knock out the rest today, before it get dark. Why? What you about to do the reason you can't take me home?"

"Shit. Kick it with this nigga. I think I'm staying over this way tonight." I honestly didn't want to go back to the condo to night, because I knew I'd be bored out my damn mind. Eliza didn't know it, but I hadn't stayed there in a week. I'd been staying in the hood, where my house was, not too far from Clarence's place. She didn't like me staying there and I wasn't going to even pretend I didn't know why.

With a roll of her eyes, she pressed her lips together and released a heavy sigh as she tried to walk out my arms. I grabbed her and wrapped them around her tighter.

"Don't act like that. I keep telling you don't shit be going down over there, Lil' Mama. A nigga just be posted. Just chilling by my damn self.

"Okay... If you say so, Alonso." I buried my head in the crook of her neck and started placing soft kisses there. "Man, I hope you don't be having hoes over there. You know these bitches be thirsty for your ass."

When she said that, I mumbled, "Man, chill out."

"Ain't no chill out. I'm serious." This time, she pulled back to look up at me. Lil' Mama wasn't smiling or anything as she looked me directly in the eyes. "I trust you, Alonso. I really do, and all I ask is that you don't make a fool out of me. Please don't do that."

I licked my lips before placing my hands on each side of her face. I tilted her head back as I leaned down, my eyes fixated on hers. "Listen, you don't have shit to worry about. I promise. A nigga just be bored and lonely at that damn condo when you're not there."

Lately, she hadn't had anything to worry about when I was at that house. Now, in the beginning, of course I was still fucking around. But the pass, I'd say, four months, I had stopped bringing females over there. I wasn't going to lie, the only reason I did was because I didn't want it getting back to her, and I knew once Eliza was out of school, she could easily pop up over there. She had before. She would get one of her little friends to drop her off and come back to get her before her curfew, but even with her having curfew, I still chose not to have anyone over there.

Trust, if I wanted to do my dirt, I had other options. I just simply wanted to do right by my Lil' Mama. The last thing I wanted to do was intentionally hurt her. Eliza was just so young and innocent and didn't deserve to be mistreated.

"Okay. I trust you." She gave me a faint smile and stretched her neck to kiss me. I parted her lips with my tongue and kissed her with everything I had in me. When the kiss ended, she mumbled, "I love you, Lonso."

"Love you, too." As the words left my mouth, the bedroom door opened, and Chyna and Clarence were walking back up front.

"You ready?" Chyna asked Eliza. Eliza nodded her head and gave me one last peck before I opened the front door so me and Clarence could walk them out.

Outside, I was hugging her when my phone vibrated in my pocket. I ignored it only for the caller to call again. Eliza pulled back and looked up at me through a raised brow, daring me to ignore this call a second time. I let her feel as if she was running shit and took it out my pocket. The last thing I needed was for her to think the person calling was someone I was fucking around with, the reason I wouldn't answer.

"Man, I don't have time for this shit," I mumbled as I sent the caller to the voicemail.

"You don't have time for what?" Eliza threw her hand on her hip and looked up at me. I didn't get a chance to answer before my phone started back vibrating in my hand.

This time, I answered.

"What, man?"

"About gotdamn time you answered. Your fucking son could be laid up here dead and you wouldn't even know because you won't answer the damn phone for me. I bet that young ass bitch don't have to call you back to back to get you to answer," my dumb ass baby mama roared on the other end. My volume was loud, so I knew Eliza heard some of what she said before I had a chance to turn the volume down.

"Man, watch yo' fucking mouth, and why would you say some dumb ass shit like that."

"Because you jump when her young ass says jump, nigga. That's why I said—"

"I'm talking about what you said about my son. Fuck that other bullshit you were spitting."

"Because I was calling to tell you that he's in the hospital, but your stupid ass—"

I cut her off. Hearing my son was in the hospital grabbed my full attention. "What hospital?"

"You don't fucking care because if you did, you would've answered when I called you the first time, and I even texted your slow ass. That bitch got your ass that fucked up that you can't even answer the phone for me? For me, Lonso! The mother of your child!" She paused to let out a chuckle. I took that as an opportunity to ask her again what hospital my son was in. "You figure it out. You should've answered when I called the first time." With that, the stupid ass girl hung up in my face.

I know it might've been wrong for a man to say he couldn't stand his baby mama, but that bitch got on my damn nerves. Nicole and I had a love/hate relationship, and right now, it was leaning more on the hate side. Every time I started fucking with someone new, she would throw a damn tantrum, knowing damn well the love I had for her was dead and gone. Yes, I loved her as the mother of my child, but I was no longer in love with her. That shit had died a long time ago.

"What's going on?" Eliza asked me, her voice laced with concern. I didn't have to bring my face up from the phone for her to see the mug displayed on my face, because one thing I knew for sure, her and the other two mothafuckas in this yard could see the steam coming from my ears.

I was too busy pulling up my message thread to answer her.

I was so fucking pissed right now that when she touched me, I shoved her away with my arm. I regretted it as soon as I did, and when I looked up at her, she had a frown plastered on her face, indicating she didn't appreciate my reaction.

"My bad, shawty." I apologized. "I don't know what the fuck is going on. The stupid bitch just called and said my son is in the hospital but won't tell me which one he's at."

Clarence asked, "Damn. Did she say what happened to Lil' homie?"

"Nah, but I'm about to go find some fucking answers. I'll get up with you later on, man." I told Clarence before looking down at Eliza, who was standing there still looking pissed. I leaned down to kiss her lips, but she quickly turned her face, causing my lips to land on her cheek. I didn't even say shit to her about that shady shit. I already had enough to deal with, and I didn't need her attitude about some shit I had done out of reflex and apologize about. "Man, whatever."

That was all I said as I jogged to my car with my phone glued to my ear. When I got inside, I took one last look at Eliza as she was getting inside Clarence car and shook my head. She was being childish as hell, and when I found out what in the hell was going on with my boy, I was letting her know I didn't appreciate that shit. I was a grown ass man, and I didn't have time for her childish ass games at a time like this. Yeah, I shoved her off me, but it wasn't like I had done it intentionally, and it damn sure wasn't in a way to hurt her.

"What's up, Auntie? Can you call that stupid ass girl and see what hospital she's at?"

"What stupid ass girl?" My Aunt Mae asked me. I had called her because she was Nicole's godmother, and I figured she could talk some sense into her ass like she had many times before. Nicole's mama and my aunt were best friends and had been for years. My mama on the other hand, she couldn't stand Nicole or her mama, and she barely liked my aunt because of her dealing with that family.

When we all were younger, my mama had walked in on Nicole's mama having sex with her boyfriend. From what I heard, my mama beat the breaks off that lady, and to this day, she couldn't stand her ass.

Why she hated Nicole for what her mama did, I honestly didn't know, but when she found out I was fucking around with Nicole, she even stopped speaking to me for a few weeks, saying I betrayed her. I guess she had a reason to be mad, but like I told her, Nicole didn't have shit to do with what her mama and her boyfriend, at the time, had done to her. Just like me, she was young and innocent to all that. However, my mama always made it a point to tell me that Nicole was going to be a hoe just like her mama.

Now, I wouldn't call her a hoe, but she damn sure had hoe tendencies.

"Nicole's dumb ass! She just called and told me that AJ was in the hospital, but she wouldn't tell me which one because I was busy when she called and didn't answer the fucking phone for her."

"What? That damn girl... Let me call Shug and see what's going on. I'll call you right back." After I said okay, we ended the call. Shug was Nicole's mama. She was in her late forties but didn't look a day over thirty. She was one of those grandparents that still thought they were young. I didn't know why, but I was headed to Nicole's house when Aunt Mae had finally called me back. "He's at Egleston. I just talked to Shug."

"Egleston? What the fuck happened to him?"

"He fell off his bike. They think his arm is broken. He was holding it crying and said he couldn't move it." Even though that shit was bad for a six-year-old, I breathed a sigh of relief, because it could've been a lot worse. "Now when you get there, don't even say shit to Nicole, because you know how she is, and I know she is about to be extra because I heard her in the background when I was talking to Shug."

"Fuck that, Auntie. I'm sick of that damn shit."

"Don't be like that, Lonso. Do I need to meet you up there?"

"Nah, if I'ma get someone to meet me up there, it's gonna be my mama so she can drag their asses." She tried telling me to calm down before saying she was about to meet me there. I told her she didn't have to again, but she hung up in my face. I could easily get my mama out of jail if she went, but the point was, I didn't want her to go, and that's the only reason I hadn't been told her about the foul shit Nicole was on when it came to my son.

She was an evil bitch, and I knew it was only going to be a matter of time before I laid hands on her, and I wasn't talking about roughing her up like I used to do. I was talking about actually beating her ass like she was a nigga.

Pulling up to the hospital, I found a parking spot where the emergency room was and hopped out. I was rushing inside when Nicole barged out.

"You better not have brought that fucking girl with you." She walked up in my face and said.

"Man, get the fuck out my face." I tried walking around her, but she stepped in my way, blocking my path. "Nicole, I'm not fucking playing with you. Let me go in there and see what's up with my son."

"No! Not until you tell me if you got that lil' hoe with you." I didn't say shit as I wiped my hand down my face and blew out a deep breath. All the while, I counted to ten in an attempt to calm myself down. "Anything you wanna know. You can ask me. I'm his mama."

"Yo', what the fuck is yo' gotdamn problem?"

"You! You my fucking problem, Lonso." Just that quick, a single tear eased down her face from her right eye, confusing the fuck out of me. "You think you can just bring another bitch to my house and I be okay with it? It's one thing to have her around my son, but to bring her to my house. That's a whole different level of disrespect, Lonso."

I licked my lips as I threw my head back, not even believing she was still upset about that bullshit. Closing my eyes, I asked God why I was stuck with this bipolar ass woman. Why did he place her in my life, but most of all, why did he pick her to be the mother of my kid? I didn't want to deal with this bullshit for the next twelve years, when my son turned eighteen.

"You know how I feel about you, and for you to play me like that..."

"Nicole, I didn't play you." I cut her off, frowning in confusion. "Fuck is you talking about. If anything, you played yourself."

"Really?" She shouted. "I played myself?" Her index finger dug deep into her chest.

"Yeah, you always play the fuck out of yourself. How many times have I told you that you need to move the fuck on because we'll never be back to where we were?"

"But I know you don't mean that shit, though." Nicole took a step closer to me and I took one back from her. "You never mean that, Lonso."

All I could do was suck my teeth and shake my head. I wasn't even about to do this shit with Nicole right now. All I wanted to do was find out what in the hell was going on with my son, and I was so thankful when my aunt walked up, because then I knew I would get my answer.

"Lonso, what's going on? Are you good?" Aunt Mae walked up and asked me. Nicole quickly wiped her tears as she mustered up a faint smile.

"Yeah, I'm just trying to see what's up with AJ." By now, Aunt Mae was closer to us, standing right beside me. When I asked Nicole how AJ was, my aunt turned to look at her, awaiting her answer right along with me.

"He's good. Just a broken arm. They wanted to run a CT scan to make sure he didn't have a head tremor or anything, being that he wasn't wearing a helmet when he fell."

"How did he fall? I mean, he must've been going pretty fast for him to have broken his arm and—"

"To be honest with you, Mama Mae, I don't know what happened. All I know is, Tasha ran inside and told me that he was outside laying in the road and had fallen off his bike. He wasn't even supposed to had been in the fucking road anyways. I told them to stay in the driveway."

"And where the fuck was you?" I asked. My questioned came out a lot harsh than I'd intended for it to. I mean, the last thing I wanted it to seem was that I was calling Nicole a bad mother, because despite her fucked up ways when it came to me, she was good to AJ, and her daughter, Tasha. I'd never had to question her motherhood.

However, Nicole was offended by my question. She scowled at me and then hollered, "I was in the damn house, cooking for my kids like a mother should. That's what the fuck I was doing. If you was home like you should've been, instead of chasing a piece of young ass, then you could've been out there watching him, dummy!" With that, Nicole turned off and stormed back inside the hospital.

I was so sick of that bitch and her slick remarks when it came to Eliza. She always had something smart to fucking say, and I knew why. Her issue wasn't with Eliza. It was with me because I didn't want her ass. Yet, if it was with Eliza, she was only scared I would love a younger person more than I'd ever loved her ass.

Aunt Mae shook her head. "That girl got issues. Come on. Let's just go inside so you can see for yourself what's going on with your son."

When we got inside, I went up to the front desk and asked the status of my son. I was told that the doctor would be right out. I took a seat far from Nicole, her mama and Aunt Mae and texted Eliza. It was getting dark, so I assumed she was done helping her mama, or was at least wrapping it up. By the time I hit send to the, *what you doing*, text, the doctor was coming out and calling for us. So, I put my phone back in my pocket because right now, my son was my main priority.

Luckily, he had just sustained a broken arm, and we were able to walk out an hour later. AJ wanted to ride home with me, and Nicole was sure to tell me that I better had took him straight home and not tried no slick shit, like I was some kidnapper or some shit. I swear, sometimes she said the dumbest shit ever.

After getting his booster seat out her car, I strapped my lil' man up and followed his mama to her house, the house I once lived in before I got tired of the fussing and fighting and packed my shit up and moved out. Even though I still had the house in the hood that I had before we decided to move in together, I didn't move back there and got my condo instead. Nicole and me only stayed together for two years before I'd had enough of her shit. I even moved back in there twice after that, but shit was never the same, and I told her the last time I moved out I wasn't moving back in there.

I didn't know if that house was bad luck or what, but I didn't want to live there.

"Come on, man. Can you walk, or you need me to carry you?" I chuckled as he stretched his arms out for me to pick him up. He had fallen asleep before I could even make it fully out the parking lot, so I wasn't tripping. Inside, I asked Nicole where she wanted me to put him and she only pointed to his bedroom.

"Go in your room, Tasha. I need to talk to Lonso right quick," Nicole ordered her daughter.

"Yes, ma'am... Goodnight, Lonso, in case I don't see you before you leave."

"Goodnight, baby girl." I wrapped my arms around her in a fatherly manner. I had been in her life since she was born, and although her father was still a part of it, I still treated her as if she was my kid. I mean, we lived under the same roof, so it wasn't like I was going to be bogus and do for my son and not her. No, she didn't get half the shit that AJ got, but she damn sure got half, especially when I lived with them.

"Can you close the door behind you, please?" Nicole said when I walked into her bedroom.

"Man, I'm not about to do this shit with you, girl. Just say whatever the fuck it is you have to say."

"Fine. I'll close it, then." She closed it and stood in front of it. She tried to be discreet and lock the door, but I heard it and asked her what in the fuck was she doing. "When are you going to stop with the games, Lonso?"

"Man, what damn games, Nicole. Look, that's what you trying to talk to me about? If it is, you can get yo' ass from in front of the door so I can go. I'm not doing this shit with you tonight."

"Yes, I wanna talk about this. I want my family back." She reached out and grabbed the front of my shirt, pulling me to her. "I miss us... I miss you, and I want you to come home."

My head shook. I wasn't moving back in here, and I'd already let her know that one too many times. "Shawty, what did I tell you the last time I moved out this bitch?" I asked and answered for her. "I told you that I wasn't moving back in here."

"But why? I know you still love me, Alonso. Come on now, don't act like that." Her voice was laced with an ounce of attitude when she said the last part. Sure, I did love her. Nothing or no one would ever change that. Not even her fucked up ways. But I wanted to love her from a distance, with her living in her house, and me in mine. I wanted to continue loving her as, she was the one that gave me my first born—my first son, and that was it. I wasn't in love with Nicole, and probably never will be again.

"I never said that, but I'm not moving back in here. All this back and forth shit is getting old. Shit be good in the beginning but in a month or two we're back fussing and shit. I'm tired of that bullshit, and you should be to."

She had the nerve to say, "Well, stop cheating on me and then we would be good."

"Nah, we cheated on each other the last time. You fucking niggas all in the club and shit, not knowing I was there." This time, Nicole sucked her teeth and dropped her head. "You can't even look at me when I bring that back up."

"It was one time that I cheated on you, Lonso. Are you going to hang that over my head forever? How many times have you fucked other bitches on me? You even cheated on me when I was pregnant with your son, but you don't see me bringing that up." I ran my tongue over my bottom lip, eyes still locked with hers as my only response was a shake of my head. I didn't want to do this with Nicole.

The way I saw it, our relationship shouldn't have even been a damn topic.

Then I said, "Look, man, I gotta go. I'll be back in the..."

This damn girl grabbed the front of my jeans and pulled me closer to her front, as she stood on her tiptoes and placed her lips on me. The shit pissed me clean off, but not once did I attempt to pull back. I was stuck, and it wasn't because I was shocked or anything like that, but it was just... no matter how upset I was with her, she still had a way to get my dick to stand. It had been a while since I had actually fucked someone, and right now, as bad as I knew it was, she had convenient pussy that she was trying to give up, but this shit was wrong... wrong as fuck and I knew it.

Yet, I couldn't even pretend the softness of Nicole's lips and the warmth of her tongue in my mouth didn't cause my dick to stand.

Placing my hands on each side of her, I pressed the palm of my hands against the door, as she fumbled with my belt buckle, unfastening my jeans. All I kept telling myself was how wrong this shit was, and how I shouldn't be doing this to Eliza. She was just so fucking innocent, and I didn't need to put her through no bullshit because I knew for a fact that Nicole liked to rub shit in mothafuckas face. I knew that firsthand, but I still couldn't stop her as she now dropped down to her knees.

The minute I felt her hot breath on my dick, I sucked in all the air I could at the time and didn't release it until the head of my dick hit the back of her throat. Her mouth was so warm and wet. See, the difference between Nicole and Eliza, Nicole wasn't new to sucking dick. This girl had been in the game for a long ass time, so she was pretty much a pro with her shit. Eliza on the other hand, my dick was the only one that had ever been in her mouth. She was good at what she did, and she sucked my shit to my liking. All Lil' Mama wanted to do was please me, and that's why I felt bad as a mothafucka right now.

Reaching down, I pulled Nicole up as I took a step back from her. As she stood, looking at me confusedly, I desperately wanted to pull my pants up and get the fuck out her house, but I fucking couldn't. The devil on my left shoulder wouldn't allow me to. So, I reached over and grabbed her by the neck, pushing her back against the door.

Through a venom filled voice, I told her, "You better not go running yo' mouth about shit that happens tonight. I shouldn't even be doing this bullshit."

Nicole smiled wide. I could see the sneakiness in her eyes, but my dumb ass chose to ignore it. "Your secret is safe with me."

I knew it wasn't... I fucking knew it, but thinking with the wrong head, I allowed myself to get lost in her world. For this one night only, Eliza or no one else was nowhere near on my mind.

6

Eliza Brown

"Eliza, get your ass up! It's almost seven." I heard my mama beating on my door. I was well aware of what time it was. Hell, I had turned my alarm off when it chimed the first time, because school was nowhere near on my mind.

Continuing to lay on my back, staring up at the ceiling, I asked her through a yell, "Can I stay home today?"

"What?" When I asked that, I heard her fumbling with the door handle. "Open this door!" Blowing out a frustrated breath, I slowly flung back the covers and crawled out of bed. I was exhausted, mentally and physically, and I knew had I gone to school it would've certainly been a waste of time. With all that was on my mind, there was no way I was going to be able to focus on my schoolwork. "What's wrong with you, La-La?"

I could tell by the way my mama was looking at me that she was thinking the worst. As I turned back around and headed back over to get in bed, I eased her mind as I said, "And I'm not pregnant. I have a headache that won't go away, and my stomach is cramping."

I silently thank God that it was about time for me to start my period. My mama knew when it was that time of the month, I had the worst stomach pain.

"Okay... You can stay. I don't think I have any more Tylenols in there, but I can bring you some when I get off or have your grandmama to bring you some over here." With the covers thrown over my head, I told her that I would be alright until she got home.

The last thing I needed was for my grandmama, which was her mama, to come over here asking a thousand and one questions. My grandmama was nosey, but a sweetheart at the same time. That lady would come over here and act like I was in bed dying. She would make me soup, start cleaning my room and all. I knew that because she'd done it before.

"Okay. I'm about to go in there and get dressed. I'll be back in here to check on you before I leave." With that, she walked out, closing my door behind her.

Still with my head underneath the cover, I reached out for my phone to text my girls in our group chat, mainly Chyna to let her know that I wouldn't be in school today because I knew she would be looking for me. When she asked why, I simply lied and told her because I wasn't feeling good. Yes, my stomach was cramping, but it wasn't nowhere near how it usually would be, because I still had a week before my cycle officially came on.

Putting my phone down, I closed my eyes and didn't even realize I had dozed off until I heard my mama calling my name, telling me that she was leaving. After we said our goodbyes and she left, I tried going back to sleep but couldn't. It wasn't long before I had sat up, threw my back against the headboard and just stared down at the text on my phone. It was from Alonso, telling me to have a good day at school and he loved me.

Love, my ass.

I wanted to call him—wanted to actually call and ask what his definition of love was, because it clearly wasn't the same as mine. However, I didn't bother. I just threw my phone to the foot of the bed, flung the covers back and got up to go shower and put on some clothes.

Once I was done, I called up my girl Zola, and she came right over. Oddly, she had stayed the night at home and pulled up in her mama's car. I was in the living room laying on the couch when she got here.

"What's up, boo? How you feeling?" Zola asked when I let her in. She was referring to the text I'd sent, telling them I wasn't feeling well and was staying home today.

"Not at all fucking good." Grabbing my phone off the floor beside the couch I'd been laying on, I pulled up Alonso's message thread and passed the phone to her.

Zola immediately frowned as she looked at the picture that I made sure was on the screen before I handed her the phone. "Who bed he's in?"

"That's what I wanna fucking know!" I pressed my lips together as I stared at her as if she had the answer I was looking for. "I wouldn't be scared to bet that it's his baby mama, though, and the bitch made it a point to send that picture to me. I didn't tell you, but the other day when I went over there, the crazy hoe tried to fight me."

"What?" Zola yelled. "See? I knew that shit was going to happen. He don't need to be taking you to that girl's house."

"I know..." I rolled my eyes. That's why I didn't even tell her about it when it first happened because I knew she would fuss. Now, I didn't even care. It is what it is. "I know, but look, why the bitch going to call Lonso, *her* nigga." I emphasized the word her.

"Her nigga? What the hell she mean?"

"Who you asking? He claimed he didn't know why she said that, but judging from this picture—"

"How do you even know it's her?" Zola cut me off. "Did you ask him who house he was at? I mean, clearly, we can tell it's a girl because of the pink sheets—"

"And her long lime green ass nails that she made sure was in the picture." I wasn't trying to hear anything Zola said. This was Alonso's baby mama, and I knew it. "Who else would do this shit? I'm not beefing with anyone else when it comes to him. So, it had to have been her. Then she sent it from his phone in the middle of the night. That only meant one thing, his ass stayed the night over there."

"Well, you told me last night that something happened to his son. Do you think that's why he stayed over there?"

I was already shaking my head before she could even finish her sentence good. Hell no... I didn't think this shit had something to do with his son, and she was crazy if she thought it did. Whether AJ was hurt or not, I wasn't giving this nigga the benefit of the doubt, and I damn sure wasn't going to believe he was anywhere other than his baby mama's house. That bitter ass bitch sent me that picture to let me know that Alonso was *her nigga,* like she said he was.

Ugh. I was so mad that I wanted to fucking fight right now, and not just anybody. Hell, not even Nicole, but her sorry ass baby daddy.

Imagine my face when I got a text from my man's phone of him in a bed that wasn't his. The same damn man that I had been calling up until I'd finally gone to sleep, to check on his son. When I saw I had a picture message from his phone, I thought maybe he'd sent a picture of AJ, letting me know that he was doing okay. Instead, it was something I damn sure wasn't expecting.

"Call him." Zola passed me the phone. "Call him and ask him about this damn picture. Clearly he doesn't know she sent it from his phone because ain't no way he's going to send you a good morning text if he knew."

She had a point, but I didn't want to ask him over no damn phone. I wanted to be face to face when I asked, and that's why I told his ass to come over to my house and call when he got outside so I could come out. There was no way that I was letting his ass come up in here. Whether I was home alone or not, I wasn't risking my life by letting him inside.

"This nigga really think he is about to come over here on some lovey dovey shit."

"And that's the funny thing about it." I said, looking back at Zola when she stated the obvious. I was standing at the screen door with my phone in my hand, waiting for Alonso to pull up. When I texted him, he texted right back, letting me know that he was actually close by, so he would be pulling up soon. I didn't bother asking what he was doing on my side of town, for two reasons. Number one, his ass was well known in the streets of Atlanta, so he knew some of everybody. Number two, his whereabouts were the least of my concerns.

In my hand, my phone chimed, and it was a text from Alonso, telling me to come outside. The whole time I walked to his car, I told myself to only ask him about the picture and that was it. However, when I pulled it up on my phone, the minute I stepped off my porch, I became pissed more than I was when it was first sent to me—which then, it was more so of a hurtful feeling that rushed throughout my body. A hurtful feeling because here I was, worried about his son and he was laid up. I was hurt beyond words, and silently cried while looking at the picture.

But now... I was pissed.

When I got to Alonso's car and he let down his window, grinning and shit, thinking I was going to lean inside and give him a hug and kiss like I'd done before, I mushed his ass in the face with my phone.

"Whoa, what the fuck you doing?" Alonso leaned over to get the phone out his face.

"No, nigga, what the fuck was you doing last night? What the hell is this, Lonso?" Being that he was now away from the phone, I was pretty sure he had a full glimpse of the picture before my screen went black.

"Man, get that shit out my face." He leaned back up as I took my hand out the car to see that my phone had went off, but it wasn't no thing for me to press the button on the side and let the front camera recognize my face so the picture could pop right back up. Stretching my arm right back out, I put the phone back in his face. This time, he knocked it away. "La-La..." He called my name in a calm voice, realizing he had fucked up.

"La-La, what? Unless you about to tell me what bitch house you were at last night, don't call my fucking name." He didn't say anything, and his silence egged me on more. "It was that bitch's, wasn't it? While you were supposed to have been with your son, magically your dick ended up in between her legs. Huh? Is that what happened, Lonso?"

I didn't have to call her name for him to know who I was referring to, he damn well knew, and because I knew he did, I was unable to hold my composure any longer. I dived my upper body into his car and started swinging on his ass. When he quickly grabbed my swinging arms, I started trying to bite him. His face. His chest. His arms. His hands. Anywhere. I just wanted to fuck him up, knowing damn well I couldn't. Alonso was a big muscular man compared to me, and it wasn't shit that I could do with my hands that would physically harm him, but I wanted him to hurt. Hurt the same way he had me hurting.

"Let me go, Alonso!" I screamed, not even caring who in the hell heard me, or what they thought was going on. For all I gave a damn, they could've called the police on his black ass.

"I'm not letting you go until you calm the fuck down." His voice was laced with venom. "You think I'm about to let yo' ass go so you can try to swing on me? You gotta be out yo' fucking mind." He spoke like he didn't deserve these licks and like I could actually hurt him.

I was no longer trying to fight him as my chest continued heaving up and down from the pants I was taking.

"Get off me!" I was damn near inside his car with only my feet dangling outside of it.

In my mind, I was going to fuck him up.

"Nawl, shawty. You need to calm down." This cheating ass son of a bitch started kissing all over my face and neck, tasting my tears and all, and it only made me cry so much harder. At the same time, it calmed me. Alonso felt my body relax because he let my arms go and wrapped his arms around my body. He whispered in my ear, "Can you just ride with me to take him home so we can talk. I just wanna talk to you."

My head shook. Lord knows I wanted to say no, but the word just wouldn't come out. I wanted to tell Alonso to go straight to hell, but that wouldn't come out either. I felt weak... so damn vulnerable. And when he kissed me on the lips and whispered, *please*, into my ear, my head nodded up and down.

"You need to go lock up your house?" Again, I nodded. I had no words for him. I was so freakin' upset, but I wanted to hear what he had to say. How in the hell he was going to justify his action—justify the picture being sent to my phone. I wanted to hear it all, and from him.

When I finally got out the car, I walked back inside my house where Zola was impatiently waiting for me. I knew she was thirsty for me to tell her what was said, and I knew she saw me trying to fight his ass. Even so, I didn't give her a chance to say anything because as soon as I walked in, I told her, "I'm about to ride with him to take his friend home. I'll call you when I get back."

My tone was dismissive, and I knew she'd gotten the hint but chose to ignore it. "What he say?" She asked when I walked back up front with my house keys in my hand.

"Nothing, really."

"So, you just went out there and jumped on him? Where ya'll about to go?" I shrugged, indicating I didn't know—which, I didn't know anything other than to take his friend home. "I don't know, La-La. He's not going to do nothing but feel you a bunch of bullshit. I wouldn't go with his ass. Let him go back to the bitch whose bed he was in."

For a minute, I just scowled at her. Not because of what she'd said, but because I wasn't strong enough at the moment to tell Alonso that.

"Don't let this man make you weak, La-La. He was just in bed with another woman, and you have the proof on your phone. Please don't let him try and feel you a bullshit ass story like he wasn't."

"I'm not!" I said with an attitude. "I just wanna hear him out. Can I do that?"

Zola picked up on my attitude and threw her hands in the air. She shook her head at me and just walked out the door, without saying anything back—which, I wasn't so sure that I wanted her to. I didn't want or need to hear how weak I was being right now. But there was nothing wrong with me wanting to hear the truth, was it?

After locking up, I walked outside as the passenger door swung open and out stepped the tall brown skinned guy. He held the door opened and said, "Here you go, queen."

I got on in the car and didn't even acknowledge him.

"Here," Alonso said as he passed my phone to me. It had fallen when I was trying to fight him. I snatched it out his hand without even looking at his ass. Yet, out the corner of my eye, I could see him rub his hand down his face as he pulled off. Although he was speeding, I didn't bother putting on my seatbelt. To be honest, it wasn't even on my mind. That freakin' picture was. He was. What I would say to him once we dropped his friend off. Honestly, I just wanted today to be over with.

I wanted to hear what he had to say so he could drop me back off at home. I was so tired that I just wanted to sleep the day away. Since I got that picture, I had been up bawling my eyes out. I was tired of thinking about it. Tired of visualizing my man making love to someone else, when he didn't even want to make love to me.

Through a chuckle that was filled with so much hurt, I mumbled, "Now I see why you so hell bent on not touching me."

"What?" I didn't have to turn my head to look at him in order to know that he was looking at me. I could feel his eyes piercing a hole through my body. We were at a stop sign, so he had a little time to give me a death stare.

"You heard me!" This time, I turned my head to look at him. If, *feeling bold*, was a person, it damn sure would've been me right now. Shit, bold wasn't even the word. "You can't fuck me, but you can lay up in some other bitch's house and—"

When I said that, Alonso reached over and tried covering my mouth with his hand. I slapped that shit right out my face.

"Don't touch me! What? You don't want your friend to know that you won't—"

This time, he reached over and mushed my head, causing it to hit the passenger window. I got on his ass when he did that. It first started with a simple slap across the chest, but when he shoved me again, I got on my knees and went to work on his ass. Punching. Scratching. Biting. I was doing it all and didn't feel bad about it.

It took the guy in the back seat to lean up and grab me.

"Man, ya'll chill the fuck out," he said, wrapping his arms around the seat and me.

"Man, get the fuck off her, King. She good." Even though Lonso was talking to his homeboy, his eyes were still locked on mine. We both were breathing hard, glaring at one another. "Just shut the fuck up, La-La. Damn. I told you we'll talk about this shit when we drop this nigga off."

"You shut the fuck up!" I jumped at his ass. The guy in the back seat, King, snickered and let me go. Alonso didn't even entertain me as he pulled off from the stop sign. The rest of the ride to drop King off, neither of us said anything. Even when King got out and said he would fuck with Alonso later, Alonso didn't say anything as his eyes remained straight ahead on the road, as did mine.

When he pulled off, he turned up the music, blasting it as I sat in the passenger seat, looking straight ahead. I knew we weren't going in the direction of my house, and like a fool, I allowed this man to take me across town to his damn condo, knowing I shouldn't have.

Neither of us said a thing as we got out and walked inside. Alonso was walking ahead of me while I kept my distance from him. Even on the elevator, I was on one side and he was on the other. It wasn't until we got inside that he grabbed me and pulled me into his arms, aggressively. Picking me up, he placed one of his strong arms around my body as he grabbed the back of my head and started kissing me. The kiss was hard and rough, and I kissed him just as hard.

It was so much hostile, yet, passion in the kiss.

I was hungry for this man. My body craved him when it shouldn't have. I wanted him to take me, all of me, and I wanted all of him. Don't get shit twisted, I was still upset, but I couldn't help the ache my body felt for him. The way it yarned for him was indescribable, and as crazy as it sounded, I wanted Alonso more now than I ever had before.

7

Alonso Davis

I was beating the fuck out of Nicole's ass. My dumb ass couldn't even believe her ass had done that bogus ass shit, but it was my fault, and I took full responsibility for it. I had not only been stupid enough to fuck her, but I slipped up and went to sleep afterwards. That's where I fucked up, and I didn't even know the crazy hoe that even got my phone. When I had finally got up around three a.m., I didn't see no miss call or anything from Eliza. So, I figured she was still pissed about me shoving her at Clarence house.

When she'd gone in her house to lock up, I got her phone and that's when I saw that the damn picture was sent from my phone. Nicole was slick as hell. She had sent the damn picture and then deleted it so I wouldn't know. I had to give her that. I was indeed pissed, but a part of me was happy as fuck because it only gave me one more reason to not fuck with her again. Even if this shit didn't work out with Eliza, I still wouldn't stick my dick back up in her snake ass.

My Lil' Mama didn't deserve this shit, and now I had to go the extreme to make it up to her—to try and mend her broken heart.

Laying Eliza down on the bed, I hovered over her, never breaking our kiss. My right hand found its way in between her legs as I rubbed her pussy through the leggings she had on. I could tell she was turned on by the way she was rotating her hips against my hand. Suddenly, I stopped and stood up. As I looked down at her, I licked my lips as she stared back up at me through anticipating eyes. She wanted me, just as bad as I wanted her. But what fucked me up were the tears escalating from her eyes, rolling down the side of her face.

I just wanted to kiss those shits away. To tell her I loved her, and I would never do anything to hurt her again. *Fuck.* I'd fucked up bad, and—and just wanted to fix it.

I pulled my shirt over my head as my tongue ran across my bottom lip before I tucked it in. My eyes were fixated on Eliza's as I unfastened my belt buckle, followed by unsnapping my jeans, allowing them to fall to the floor. As I stood with only my boxer briefs and socks on, I waited for her to make any kind of gesture like she didn't want this, but I knew she did. It was written on her face, as well as in her teary eyes. When she didn't say anything, I reached for the hem of her leggings and slowly pulled them down, as well as the black silk underwear she wore.

As Eliza laid bottomless, I pulled my dick out my briefs and then positioned myself in between her legs. She wrapped her arms around my neck as her legs spread wider. We shared a passionate kiss as I took my right hand and placed it between our midsection, grabbing my dick. I started rubbing the head of it through her split, wetting her pussy more than it already was. I wasn't going to even lie, the warmness of her pussy felt good on my dick, and I couldn't wait to push my shit inside of it.

"Ssssss," Eliza's body tensed up as she made a hissing noise and squeezed my neck tighter. I wanted to ask if she wanted me to stop, but I was too afraid she'd say yes. So, I just covered her mouth with mine as I continued, slowly, forcing myself inside of her entrance. "Ahhhhh... Sssssssss." Her cries were low and so innocent like.

This wasn't the way I visualized myself taking her innocence, but with the head of my dick already inside, I'd be damn if I was stopping now. I buried my head in the crook of her neck and could feel the tears still trickling down the side of her face. At this point, I didn't know whether Eliza was crying from still being upset and hurt by my fuck up or crying from the pain I knew she was feeling at the moment, from my dick.

"Damn..." I grunted. I was in. My whole dick was inside of Eliza and the shit felt damn good. She was warm and so fucking wet. She was ready, and it showed when she started slowly moving her hips while letting out soft moans in my ear. I started matching her rhythm as I whispered how good her pussy felt. My whole twenty-five years of living, I had never taken anyone's virginity, because that wasn't my style. I didn't want no inexperience woman, but here I was, taking Eliza's. I knew after this shit, there was no way I could hurt her again. She was mine, and I damn sure was hers.

"Oh my god, Alonso. It feels so good."

I let my kisses trail from Eliza's neck, along her jawline, to her mouth. I started giving her pecks and before I knew it, my thrust had become a little more forceful as I asked her, "Was this what you wanted? Huh? Am I giving you what you want? You wanted some dick, right?"

She nodded as she cried out, "Yes." I looked down into her face and noticed she had her eyes closed tightly. Her mouth was wide open, and she had a pleasurable look on her face. Yet, it was filled with pain.

"Look at me. Please, baby. Look at me." I couldn't tell you if she looked at me or not, because as soon as I told her to, I leaned down and started kissing her. The kiss held so much passion in it. I was sorry for hurting her and wanted her to know that. "Please... Please don't fucking leave me. I love you so much, man. Fuck. I love you, Eliza."

Yeah, I knew I was admitting to cheating, but right now, I didn't give a damn. I just didn't want Eliza to give up on us.

I felt her body shaking underneath me as she whimpered in my ear. All the while, she hugged me tighter and buried her face in the crook of my neck, breathing hard and still crying. After what felt like forever, she finally said the words that caused me to reach my peak.

Her moans grew louder as she said, "I love you too, Alonso. I promise I'm not going anywhere."

That shit had a nigga rushing to pull out of her. I could've nutted in her and knocked her ass right up, but I knew that would've only been selfish on my part. Sure, I wanted her to be mine for the rest of my life, but I knew a baby wouldn't make that happen. Plus, Eliza was so damn young, and I didn't even want to tie her down like that. When or if we had a baby, I wanted the time to be right, and clearly it wasn't right now.

"Fuck... Damn." I fell on side of her, panting. She turned on her side, snuggling her body against mine as she laid there breathless as well. I wrapped my arms around her, pulled her in closer than she already was. Stretching my neck downward, I kissed the top of her head as I asked, "You okay?"

"Yes," her voice was low and raspy. "What time is it?"

I looked over at the clock on the nightstand and told her that it was noon and asked what time she had to be home. She let me know she wanted to at least be there by four being that her mama got off at six, and she didn't want her to think she stayed out of school to lay up. That was understandable. I mean, I wasn't trying to get shawty in any kind of trouble.

"Let me go get you a towel," I said and didn't wait for her to respond as I slid off the bed. I was in the bathroom wetting a towel when Eliza walked in and called my name.

She said, "I need to get in the shower, and... and I messed up your bed." Her voice was so low that I barely heard her when she said, "I'm bleeding."

"Damn, really?" I said as I walked out the bathroom to see. "It's alright. You can get in the shower. I'll change the sheets." She nodded and closed the bathroom door. While she was inside, I was changing the sheets. In the mix of doing that, my phone vibrated on the floor in my pants pocket. When I got it, I saw it was a call coming in from Nicole's phone. I fought with myself on whether I should answer the phone or not. It could've been my son, but because I didn't want to risk the chance of it being his dumb ass mama, I didn't even bother answering it.

I sent the caller to the voicemail and turned my phone off. I didn't have time for the stupid shit. I only had a little more time to spend with Eliza before it was time to take her home, and I wanted to give her my full attention. I just prayed it wasn't my son calling.

"You good?" I asked Eliza when she walked out the bathroom. She had a towel wrapped around her body as she slowly walked into the room. She looked so stressed, and her eyes were puffy. I felt so fucking bad that I could've kicked my own ass right now. "Come here." I pulled her into my arms and kissed the top of her head. Backing back, I took a seat on the bed and pulled her on my lap. It fucked me up that she couldn't even look at me, but I grabbed her chin and made her. "I love you, Eliza, but I fucked up. I fucked up big time, and I know no amount of apology could fix what I'd done, but I do love you, and I'm not trying to lose you."

By the time I finished talking, she had tears streaming down her face. "Why? Why did you do it, Alonso? If you were that hard up for some pussy, you could've fucked me." She hopped off my lap. Just like that, she had a mug on her face like she was about to swing on my ass again. "How long have I been throwing my shit at you? I been trying and trying to please you, but you go out and let some other bitch do it instead. The same bitch that hates my ass. The same ass hoe that stood in my face and called you her nigga. Really, Alonso?" She pounded her fist against the palm of her hand as she spoke, indicating that she was pissed. Nonetheless, the hurt being heard in her voice outweighed the anger.

"Man, I already told you that the shit I did didn't have nothing to do with you. And you already know why I never fucked you, La-La. You weren't ready, shawty."

"Well, you damn sure didn't think that a few minutes ago."

My head dropped and shook. Even with me just giving her some dick moments ago, I still felt she wasn't ready and that's why I didn't give her my all, but I didn't bother telling her that.

Bringing my head back up to look at her, I said, "Man, look, I didn't fuck that damn girl because I wasn't getting no pussy from you. It didn't have shit to do with you. I was thinking with the wrong head. Point blank. I'm not going to even kick it to you like I had slipped up and didn't know what I was doing—" I paused and ran my hand down my face. "I could've stopped her and walked the fuck out, but I didn't. Like I said, I was thinking with the wrong head. I fucked up and I take full responsibility for my actions."

Eliza chuckled. The chuckled was filled with hurt and disbelief. Hell, I was in disbelief with my realness, but I loved this damn girl too much to tell her a bunch of lies.

"And that's all you have to say? You fucked up?"

"What else you want me to say?" I eyed her in confusion.

"How about you sorry and it'll never happen again. You're saying everything, but that. You even said you know no amount of apology could fix what you'd done, but you have yet to say you're sorry."

"What?" I frowned. "I am, and you know that. I thought me saying I'm not trying to lose you let you know that." She didn't say anything —just continued standing there scowling at me with her arms now folded over her chest. Reaching out, I grabbed her by the arm and pulled her to me, positioning her in between my legs. She had a towel wrapped around her body and I unraveled it. I placed soft kisses on her stomach before sitting her naked body on my lap. I looked her dead in the eyes as I licked my lips and said, "I'm sorry... like, dead ass. I'm sorry and you don't have to worry about that shit happening ever again."

"Was this the first time? I mean, just the other day she called you her nigga. That's why, huh? Because you been fucking her this whole time?"

"What? Hell no! That bitch just crazy and will say anything to get under your skin." I half lied. I hadn't been fucking Nicole the *whole* time I'd been with Eliza, but a little over a month ago I did let the hoe suck my dick. Again, I was thinking with the wrong head, but I had to make sure that shit wasn't going to happen again. Like I said before, sex with Nicole was hard to turn down. I had been doing a damn good job with it until the slip up a month prior and the one just the night before.

With the bogus shit she pulled, it wouldn't be happening again.

"Well, she damn sure have a way to get under my skin." Eliza dropped her head. She was quiet for a few minutes until I asked what she was thinking. "You really wanna know?"

"Yeah." I stroked the side of her face as she brought her head up to look at me. "Yeah, I do wanna know, and be honest. If you think I'm a fuck ass nigga for doing that stupid shit, tell me."

Eliza chuckled.

"Yeah, I do think you're that." She let off another chuckle. I didn't even get mad because I knew it was the hurt running through her body that made her say that. She didn't mean it. "And, I'm thinking about how stupid I am. You cheated on me and here I am letting you take my virginity. I have to be the dumbest bitch right now, and I can only imagine what my girls going to say. Zola especially.

"Fuck them bitches!" I said that from the heart. "They don't need to say shit about what we got going on. Ya'll know too much of each other's business as it is. Well, they know yours."

"And what does that supposed to mean, Lonso?" She raised a brow as I signal for her to get off my lap. As she stood, she asked, "Huh? What does that supposed to mean?"

"It means I want you to come lay down with me." I grabbed her hand and pulled her over to the bed as she tried asking what I meant again, and again, I told her nothing as I kissed the top of her forehead. "I know you have to be at home in a minute, but I just want an hour. Can I hold you?"

"I guess..." While she rolled her eyes, I shook my head as we climbed in bed. Pulling her close to me, I kissed the back of her neck and held her tight.

8

Eliza Brown

S *hit.*

"Oh my God... Lonso, get up!" I shrugged Alonso off me
as I jumped out his bed. He was snuggled up behind me, knocked the
hell out. It was dark outside, and I knew for a fact that my mama had
beat me home, when I should've gotten there before her.

"Fuck!" Alonso leaped out the bed with me. Being that he lived on
the sixteenth floor of his building, it overlooked the city of Atlanta, so
he never closed his curtains. Whether he did it over in the night to
avoid the sunlight in the mornings, I didn't know. But I know I had
never come over and there were covering the huge windows. "Damn,
bae. I'm sorry. I fell asleep."

"Where the hell is my phone?" I looked around on the floor as I
fastened my bra. I spotted my panties laying by his bed and remembered I didn't put them back on. My mind was so messed up right
now that I wasn't even thinking about those things and left them
right on the floor. When I heard Alonso say here, I looked back to see
him holding my phone out to me. "Shit. It's dead. Oh my god. What
time is it, Alonso?"

"Bae, calm down." When he moved from in front of his nightstand, I saw that it was only eight. But still... I should've been home. "Just say you was with your homegirls or something."

"You think my mama give a damn about that? She don't even like them like that." My mama only tolerated my girls. Let her tell it, they were bad influence on me, and she only said that because while I had always had a curfew, they didn't. Chyna especially. Oh, my mama's dislike for her was strong, and Chyna knew that, too. Sometimes, she would say something to my mama just because she knew she didn't like her. "And if I tell her that I was running the streets with them, it would only make her not like them more."

"Well, what you going to tell her."

"I don't know... I can't tell her that I was with you," I smartly stated the obvious. "I'm just fucked either way."

Alonso shook his head. He had so much pity in his eyes while looking at me that it made me feel embarrassed. He was twenty-five. A grown man that wasn't used to this shit. The way I was panicking, one would've thought I was about to get my ass beat with a belt or something of that sort. While I might not had gotten beat, I damn sure wasn't ready for the words my mama had waiting for me.

I didn't want to be put out on my ass. No, I hadn't miss curfew, but I had just missed school because I wasn't feeling well—at least that's what I told my mama—but here I was, MIA when I should've been home. Erika White was one of those, *if you can't go to school, don't leave my damn house*, mothers.

"You ready?" Alonso asked me as he walked out the bathroom. He'd gone in there after giving me a pity stare down. While he was in there handling his business, I went to the living room to wait for him.

"Yeah." Getting off the couch, I followed him out the door.

Inside the car, neither, Alonso nor me said a word. I had my head pushed back against the headrest, eyes closed and hands in my lap when I felt him grabbed my left hand. I didn't bother opening my eyes as I felt him take it to his lips and place soft kisses on it.

"I'm sorry," Alonso mumbled between those kisses. I asked him what he was sorry for, and his reply was a simple, "For everything.

For hurting you. For not having you home in time. Just for everything, shawty. I'm sorry."

For a minute, I didn't say anything. I just sat here, not bothering to open my eyes, or change my posture. Not at all did I blame Alonso for me not being home, but I damn sure blamed him for the hurt that burned inside of me. I didn't blame Nicole, although I hated that bitch, but I blamed him. *Alonso.* He was the one that was supposed to not have me looking stupid. The one that wasn't supposed to break my heart.

Nicole's bitch ass didn't owe me any type of loyalty. My man did. And what did my dumb ass do? Let him take my virginity like he hadn't just betrayed me. The thought of all this pained me all over again. It made me angry, but this time, I was angrier at myself. I knew one thing; I didn't know when *that* would ever happen again. Not because there wasn't a doubt in my mind that I would be on punishment, but because I—I just didn't know if I wanted to have sex... Not with him.

I released a heavy sigh as I opened my eyes. That's when I realized I was crying. I quickly wiped the tears away as I said, "I really don't want to think about that Alonso. I mean, it is what it is."

"Nah, it ain't no, it is what it is, babe." He brought my hand back to his lips and kissed it again. I don't know why, but that annoyed me.

I wanted to snatch my hand away from him so bad, but as bad as I wanted to, I just couldn't make myself. Right now, at this very moment, I hated how much I loved this man. I wanted to unlove him. Go back to a few hours ago when I let him take my innocence, but I knew that was impossible.

Instead of snatching my hand away, I just let him continue holding it in his, as I stated, "It is what it is, because we can't change what happen. You can't go back and un-fuck her, can you? You can't go back and un-break my heart. You can't do none of that shit, Alonso. I can't get that damn image out my fucking head, no matter what you thought deleting that picture would do."

Yes, this fool had deleted the damn picture out my text, like that was going to change what I'd saw. I noticed it was gone when he gave me my phone back when I left my house with him. I wasn't going to even say anything about it, but I felt this was the perfect time to let his ass know him deleting it didn't change the fact that his hoe ass baby mama had sent it to me.

"I know it won't change the fact, but that don't mean I'm not sorry." As he was saying that, we were pulling up to the end of my street. "Can I see you tomorrow? I can pick you up from school."

"I don't know, Alonso. I mean—"

"Why? Because you're still mad?"

"No... I—I just don't know." My voice was low and hesitant. Being upset with him really didn't have anything to do with anything, because I knew my ass would've agreed the second he asked that question. I just didn't want to tell him that I knew I was going to be on punishment.

This shit was embarrassing.

Here I was, about to be eighteen in a couple of months and I was still getting treated like a child. I was a good child. I made good grades, would be graduating soon, didn't steal, never been in jail and I never came to my mama about having no STD or had gotten knocked up by some boy that I barely even knew... I was good, and I didn't deserve for her to be breathing down my damn back all the time.

Alonso let out a frustrating breath and reluctantly said, "Okay."

No matter how upset I was, I leaned over and gave him a kiss. It wasn't passionate, but it was a long press on the lips. When I pulled back from it, I noticed he was looking at me funny. I ignored it and gave him a faint smile as I turned to get out the car. As I walked the short distance to my house, so many thoughts were going through my head. Surprisedly, what I'd be walking in to when I made it home wasn't one of those thoughts. Alonso and our relationship were. I honestly didn't know where we would stand now.

Alonso was a grown man. He was used to doing grown people shit. As much as I tried to tell myself that he knew I wasn't grown when he decided to still fuck with me after my mama exposed my real age to him, he still had the right to be frustrated; especially on the nights he wanted me to stay with him. Hell, I was frustrated. I wanted to be held all night by him. I wanted to wake up to him kissing on the back of my neck while saying good morning to me, like they did on movies.

I'd always dreamed of being like the girls in the romance movies, and although I was dealing with a brother from the hood, I still felt my fairytale love story would come true. Now, with his latest stunt, I wasn't so sure it would come true.

"Go straight to your fucking room!" My mama said, startling me, the second I walked inside. "I don't wanna see you and I don't want to hear your voice, because I really have the mindset to beat your fucking ass right now, lil' girl. I don't know who the fuck you think I am. I ain't boo-boo the gotdamn fool, and I would be damned if you're going to try and play me like I am."

"Ma, I was just—"

"I don't wanna fucking hear it, and if you say another motha-fuckin' word to me, I'm going to politely get my ass up and go off in yo' shit." Shocked was an understatement, as I wondered what in the hell my mama knew about going off in somebody's shit. Yet, I didn't say anything and damn near ran to my room.

Even though she was talking calm to me, I could see in her eyes that she would live up to her threat and go off in my shit.

Inside my room, I put my phone on the charger and gathered me some clothes up so I could shower. In that shower, as I tried cleaning between my legs, it caused a smile to coat my face. The tenderness of my kitty caused me to shiver, reminding me that my boo, yes, Alonso was still my boo, had just been there hours ago. I was sore, but it was a pleasurable soreness I felt. He had worked me. Sex with Alonso was more than I expected, but it was my first time, so I really didn't know what to expect.

The only thing that disappointed me was the timing of it.

I always imagined my first time being romantic, not because my boyfriend had cheated on me and wanted to make it all go away by giving me what he knew my body had been craving. Alonso was slick. He knew damn well I wasn't going to turn down his dick, because I wanted it. I've wanted it since only a couple of weeks of us dating.

"You lucky I don't take that damn phone." I opened the bathroom door to my mama standing in her doorway. She had a cigarette in her hand, and a stressful look on her face. I was stressing her. But I wasn't even doing shit. I just wanted to live a little. I felt my mama was being too strict, and I couldn't wait until I was eighteen. I was getting a job and getting the hell out this house. "For the next two weeks, when school is out, you bring your ass straight home. I swear to God, La-La, if you're not here when I get here... I don't even want to think about what I'ma do because the shit scares me."

"Yes, ma'am." I said but didn't even know if she heard me due to her slamming her bedroom door in my face. I rolled my eyes as I released a heavy sigh that was filled with frustration. As I went into my room and shut and locked the door behind me, I had to remind myself that I would be eighteen soon, because that was the only way I didn't run away. I didn't care that I didn't have anywhere to go. I just didn't want to be in this house.

I HAD FINALLY SAW CHYNA AT LUNCH. I WAS SITTING ALONE OUTSIDE when she walked over to my table. Her Spanish accent was loud and thick when she grilled me. "Bitch, have you been trying to ignore me today? I was looking for you this morning."

She was right. I had been trying to ignore her. I knew that Zola had told her about Alonso, and I just didn't want to talk about it. Furthermore, I was embarrassed. Embarrassed that the man I thought so highly of would hurt me like that. Embarrassed that he was slowly proving everybody right. My friends, Chyna especially, said if I didn't give him some pussy, he would surely get it elsewhere. And, I guess she was right.

"No, Chyna. Why would you think I've been ignoring you?" I tried my best to sound as normal as I could.

"Because, I been looking for you all freakin' day. You weren't even at our meet up spot this morning, and I didn't think you was here until I asked Ciara and she told me you were." I didn't say anything because really, I didn't feel there was anything to be said. I was here and she saw that now. "So, what's up? What's going on with you and Alonso? Zola told me some shit had gone down, but she didn't say what. I even tried calling you yesterday and all night, but your phone was powered off. What's going on?"

My eyes rolled. This is the exact reason I was trying to ignore her. Zola should've gone on and told her the whole thing since she told her that much. Now I was forced to tell her, and I wasn't even in the mood to talk about it. I didn't want to relive the moment. The wound was still fresh, and Lord knows I didn't want to be walking around this school with puffy eyes due to me crying.

"Did he hit you?" I shook my head at her question as I frowned. Other than yoking my ass up, Alonso would never hit me. At least I didn't think he would. "Well, what's wrong?"

My head dropped. I didn't want to voice the words aloud, but Chyna was my girl, and the last thing I wanted was for her to think I was keeping secrets. We'd been telling each other everything for years. I'd never gone through boy problems, because Tyrell definitely didn't count, but Chyna had, and she told me everything. When she lost her v-card. When Spanky, her ex, had put his hands on her for the first time when she was only fifteen, she told me. So, I had to tell my girl this.

As I looked back up at her through my tears, I mumbled, "He cheated. His black ass cheated on me with his baby mama."

"Shut up!" Chyna yelled in my ear as she slapped my arm. "You're lying."

"I wish I was..." My voice cracked as I grabbed a napkin off my tray. I was dabbing at my eyes when Chyna grabbed the napkin from me and started doing what I was just doing, wiping my eyes. She looked pissed, like she wanted to find Alonso and fuck him up for what he'd done to me.

"It's okay, Mamacita. Don't cry over him. You are a beautiful black queen that doesn't deserve this shit. If he can't see that, then fuck him, but you will not cry over him. If anything, you will boss up on that nigga and show his ass who's the boss."

I let off a couple of chuckles at her. I loved when my girl was upset because her Spanish accent was so freakin' cute.

"Have he ever done this shit before?" My head shook. "Good, but don't give his ass a reason to think he can do it again. Now, I can't tell you whether you should forgive him or not, because it's your relationship and you're gonna handle it how you see fit, but don't for one second give him a reason to believe he could ever do it again. Trust me, I had to learn the hard way that once you let these brothers think they could slide, their asses start trying to ice skate, and us Queens don't have time for that."

I just stared at my girl. She was speaking the truth, and for a second, I'd almost forgot Chyna was only eighteen. She sounded so mature. I had to also remember, Chyna might've been young, but she wasn't new to the dating world. She'd had quite a few guys that she thought she was in love with, and with the shit Spanky had taken her through, my girl probably knew what she was talking about. Even so, I wanted to tell her that it was too late for that, because I'd already given Alonso the nookie.

"Anyways, so what are you doing after school? I got Clarence car. Maybe we can go get our nails done or something." My head was already shaking by the time her sentence ended. I wasn't gambling with my life by not going straight home after school. "Why not?" Chyna wanted to know.

"Girl, for two weeks, I can't go nowhere but home and school. My mama actually said if I didn't, she was going to bust me in my shit."

"What? Bust you in your shit?" What the hell did you do?" Chyna looked surprised before busting out laughing. All I did was shake my head. My mama had never said no mess like that. "Tell your mama she has to ease up. Is she going to be acting this way when you turn eighteen? I mean, damn. Threatening to bust you in your shit? That's another level of crazy. I would usually say that shit to someone on the streets, but Mrs. Erika is a straight up G. She said it to you... her daughter."

"Chyna, shut up. This shit is not funny. It's actually embarrassing."

"I bet. I mean, I get that you're still staying under her roof and she wants you home at a reasonable time, but come on now. She is putting you on punishment. Your mom is acting like the parents in those lifetime movies. They are forever putting their teen daughter on punishments." We both laughed when she said that, because it was true. "Next thing I know, you're going to be jumping out the windows to meet up with Alonso. Well, maybe not him, but some damn body."

I was still laughing as I nudged her. "Shit up, girl. I am not about to be sneaking out no damn house."

"Yeah, I bet you're not, because Mrs. Erika don't play, and I damn sure don't want her busting you in your shit." We both laughed as the bell rung and we started gathering up our stuff to head to our next class. Before we parted ways, she told me, "Meet me up front. I'll drop you off at home after school."

After saying okay, we hugged and parted ways. I could always count on Chyna to give me a good laugh.

9

Chyna Wilson

I felt so bad for Eliza. Although I was managing to keep a smile on her face, I could still see the pain in her eyes, and I didn't like that bullshit. I wanted to fuck Alonso's ass up because my girl didn't deserve to be cheated on. Eliza was the good one out of the three of us, and no, I wasn't saying Zola and I were hoes or deserved to be cheated on, because no one deserved that. It was just, you didn't meet a girl nowadays that weren't in the streets chasing dicks. Again, no, Zola and I weren't either, but our young asses had been with quite a few guys. While Zola had been with three, I'd been with five— thanks to me getting drunk and letting Tyrell and his stupid friends run a damn choo-choo train on me.

I was still disgusted with myself about that.

Anyways as far as I knew, Eliza hadn't been with anyone, if she had, she would've told me. My girl didn't sleep with this nigga and that nigga. She was a good catch, and Alonso was flat out dumb for what he'd done to her. I was so pissed about that, and as soon as I dropped her off, I was going to Clarence house and pick a fight with him. Just because his homeboy had done my girl dirty. After all, I couldn't say shit to Alonso about it.

"Well, alright, mama. This is your stop." I pulled up in front of

Eliza's house to see her mama's car parked in the driveway. "I see your mama's home. Tell her I said, hey." I laughed, knowing damn well her mama didn't like me. I didn't even know why, but let Zola tell it, Mrs. Erika thought Eliza was better than us. I mean, that might've been true, but I never looked at it like that. And, so what if she did, that was her child. She was entitled to feel that way. That doesn't mean it made it true.

"Okay, boo. Let me go in there and deal with this crazy woman. I'm about to go straight to my room, because I do not feel like hearing her mouth."

I only laughed, but I didn't blame her. Her mama nitpicked at everything.

After she got out, I wanted to ride pass my house before heading to Clarence. I didn't know why, but something told me to go the opposite way that I usually went, and when I did, the site in front of me nearly caused me to wreck Clarence's car. It was my daddy, and he was standing at a black Chevrolet Caprice, sitting on 30-inch rims—which was Clarence's fucking car. Anger automatically consumed me.

It didn't take a damn rocket scientist to know why my dad was at that car. He was on drugs while Clarence sold the shit.

Being the type that didn't overlook bullshit, I headed their way, speeding right by them. I didn't stop, but I wanted them to see me. To see me and know I saw my dad at his car. I was so upset that I no longer cared to ride by my house. I wanted to go straight to Clarence's house and be there when he got there, knowing he probably wasn't coming straight home.

When I got there, I parked his car in its usual spot, got out and went inside. Although I was upset, I was more hurt than anything. Hurt that Clarence was possibly—well, Clarence *was* supporting my dad's drug habit. He knew I hated my dad was on drugs, and I'd told him so many times that I wished he would get the help he needed. The crazy part about all this, and what pissed and hurt me the most, Clarence always comfort me and told me that my dad would have to want it for himself. The other day, he even offered to help my mom and I in any way when or if we wanted to put him in rehab.

Without my consent a tear trickled down my face. I hadn't cried in a long time, so this surprised me. I wasn't a crier. The last time I had cried was when my ex, Spanky, thought it was okay to lay hands on me every chance he got. I was young and dumb then, so I thought that was love. I'd witness my dad lay hands on my mom over the years and she stayed. So my young ass didn't know any better. It took a teacher at my school to tell me that Spanky putting his hands on me wasn't love. Like, the beating was so bad that he got bold enough to lay hands on me at school. All because he thought I was talking to some other guy.

Thinking back on that shit depressed me, and I vowed to never go out like that again. If a nigga hit me, he was going to have to kill me because I damn sure was going to try and kill his ass.

After slipping off my school close, I put on a pair of spandex shorts and a crop top and headed back up front. I decided to fix me a chili cheese dog as I waited for Clarence. I wasn't cooking shit tonight, and as far as I was concerned, his ass could eat air.

Hours had pass when Clarence finally decided to make it home. I was laid back on the couch smoking but quickly sat my ass up when I heard him fumbling with the door. What got me was him walking in and heading straight to his bedroom like he didn't see me sitting here. I jumped up when I heard the bathroom door close and decided to stand in front of it and wait for him.

He was in there a lot longer than I anticipated, but I didn't move, and when I heard the water turn on and off, I got in character.

Clarence opened the door and jumped. "Damn. You been standing there this whole time, looking crazy?"

"You gotdamn right I have!" I watched as he walked over to the bed. "How long have you been selling drugs to my dad? Huh?" I asked but didn't give him a chance to answer. "Really, Clarence? After all the nights I've cried on your shoulder about him needing to go to rehab, you sell that bullshit to him. You bogus as fuck."

"Man, who in the hell said I was selling anything to that man?" He frowned as if I didn't know the truth. "As a matter of fact, who said I even sell drugs in the first gotdamn place? The fuck."

"Please don't do that bullshit. Don't try to play me like I don't fucking know what you do. I might be young, but trust, I'm far from dumb. Now how long have you been selling drugs to my dad." I continued grilling him. When he didn't say anything, I told him once again that he was bogus for that, and I felt betrayed. He spoke up then, telling me that he didn't know what I was talking about. That angered me more. I wanted to punch him. I was so mad. "You know what, fuck it. You're full of shit, Clarence. All ya'll niggas full as shit. You just like yo' homeboy, a liar and a cheater."

"A cheater? The fuck that come from?" I didn't say anything, just stood here gawking at his ass. He was frowning in confusion. I had never come to Clarence about him cheating, so this was all new to him. "How the fuck did we go from you accusing me of selling to yo' pops to you thinking I'm cheating on yo' ass?"

My eyes rolled.

Honestly, I never had a reason to accuse Clarence of anything. I wasn't the type to snoop through his phone, so I didn't know if he was talking to other women or not, he just never showed me any signs that he was. Sure, he came home late as fuck on some days, but I knew he was a d-boy, and that was expected. And, if he was cheating, he better had prayed I didn't find out, because I would certainly fuck his ass up and leave him.

"Nawl, don't get fucking quiet on me now. You was just talking big shit." He stood from the bed and walked up on me. I stood my ground as his tall frame towered over my five-five thick self. I had gotten all my curviness from my black side of the family—which was my dad's side. All my aunts on his side were curvy. We all had a small waist, with thick thighs and a big ass. I had a banging ass body. "Now what the fuck you talking about, I'm just like my homeboy. Who the fuck you talking about?"

"Don't fucking worry about it, Clarence. Just tell me why the fuck I saw my dad at your house? How long have you known him?"

"Fuck that! That shit ain't none of your gotdamn business."

"It ain't my business?" I shouted as I threw my right hand on my hip and shifted all my weight to one side. "News flash nigga, my dad is my business."

"Well, if that nigga is your business, go ask him what the fuck you wanna know. Shit." Clarence's voice was dismissive as he walked back over to the bed and took a seat. He leaned forward, propping his elbow on his knees as he started going through his phone. I was tempted to go knock it out his hand but thought against it.

Turning around, I walked over to the closet and started gathering up my things, not even caring if Clarence thought I was overreacting or not. This shit was wrong in my eyes. *How could I be with a man that sold drugs to my dad?* I didn't want to.

Walking out the closet, I dropped my two overnight bags by the bathroom door so I could go in there and get my hygiene products. When I had all my stuff, I stood at the bedroom door with my bags on my shoulder and my books and things in my hand. Being that I didn't want Clarence to see that I was crying, I didn't even bother to turn around and look at him when I said, "Can you take me home, please?" I asked.

Clarence laughed. I'm talking about... this nigga actually looked up at me and busted out laughing, hard as fuck, too, and I knew why. Here I was, done put on a whole show by packing my bags and had to ask him for a ride home.

"Man, I'm not taking your ass no gotdamn where." My chest heaved up and down from the deep breath I'd taken as I turned to face him. When he saw me wipe my tears away, his stupid laugh ceased as he sat his phone beside him, and he reached out for me. "You really crying over this bullshit? Come here, shawty."

I allowed him to grab me and pull me in between his legs. As he wrapped his arms around my waist and rubbed my ass, he looked up at me and licked his pinkish lips before speaking.

"Yo' pops asked me not to tell you I knew him. I've known him for years, but I didn't know he was your pops, man. Dead ass. I found out the first time I took you home, and I was going to tell you then, but I didn't know if you knew the nigga was a... was on drugs or not—

which the shit is obvious." He was about to call my dad a crackhead, but he thought against it.

"But you had plenty of times to tell me. How long have we been kicking it, Clarence?"

"Yeah, you right. I could have, but yo' pops begged me not to. The nigga said he didn't want you to know we knew each other." He licked his lips again. "You know the nigga is in denial, right? He don't think he got a problem, and he got in his head that nobody know he's on that shit. Like, on some real shit, that's why I'm always telling you that he has to want it for himself. Shawty, yo' pops don't wanna get clean because he doesn't feel like he has a problem. In order to get help, one has to realize they're an addict."

"So, you're saying that he's never going to get clean? He going to be on drugs forever?"

Clarence shook his head. I didn't care that I sounded like a small child. I just wanted my dad clean before he got worse than he already was. He'd already begun stealing little shit out the house and didn't think anyone would notice. As far as I knew he still had his job, but I didn't know how long that would last.

"I'm not saying that, but I don't think it'll be no time soon. That man ain't about to walk into nobody's facility for no gotdamn help. Not willingly."

I closed my eyes as I released a heavy sigh. When I reopened them, a fresh set of tears welled in the pit of my eyes. I prayed they wouldn't fall, but my prayer fell on deaf ears. Just as quickly as they rolled down my face, Clarence reached up and wiped them away. I allowed him to, and when my tears were gone, he stretched his neck to give me a passionate kiss in an attempt to make me feel better.

10

Clarence Thomas

I hated my shawty had found out about me selling to her pops the way she had. In my defense, though, I wanted to tell her, but Henry didn't want me to. I should've known not to listen to a gotdamn crackhead. But at the end of the day, Chyna was his daughter, and I felt he knew best. After seeing the hurt in her eyes and her crying, I now regretted not telling her.

"Can I ask you something?" Chyna asked in an innocent child like voice. She was still positioned in between my legs, but her arms were now wrapped around my neck from the kiss we shared a little while ago. I told her that she could ask me anything, but I wasn't expecting the question that she asked. "Can you stop selling to my dad? Like, I like you and all Clarence, but I don't want to be with a nigga that's sells drugs to my dad. I can't and I won't be with—"

"Say less, shawty." Her ass looked surprised when I said that. I mean, it wasn't like the shit was going to make or break a nigga.

"You would really do that for me?"

I frowned. Me and Chyna hadn't used the L-word before, but shawty meant a lot to me. More than she knew. "Of course I will, shawty. I mean, I'm not tryna lose you over this shit, and it's not like I need his little money, but you do know he's not gon' do shit but find another D-boy to buy it from. Right?"

"Yeah, I know... But it won't be *my* D-boy that he gets it from." She leaned forward and pressed her soft ass lips against mine. When she pulled back, I asked was she going to go talk to her pops about this, and her reply was, "I don't really want to. I mean, I do but then I don't. Like, the shit is embarrassing. What would I say, find somewhere else to buy your drugs from?"

"All I can say is, say how you feel. I mean, he's going to find out anyways when he called me to buy some more and I tell him I can't sell to his junkie ass."

"Clarence!" Chyna hit my arm and narrowed her eyes at me. I apologized and we both laughed. Shawty had a sense of humor behind closed doors, so we always joked around. Hell, my mama was an alcoholic. So, I didn't have no room to talk. Just like I clowned her pops, she clowned my mama. "And if he do find out, so what. Either he can stop using or go to someone else."

My only response was a nod of my head as my phone vibrated beside me. While I picked it up to answer, Chyna straddled my lap and started kissing all over my neck. My hands automatically went to her ass as she rotated her hips. Off top, my dick came to life. I was ready to fuck her right here and now.

"Yo, what's up, Lonso?" I answered for my nigga. Me and Alonso had been cool since knee-high. Believe it or not, that nigga and me had never fallen out over anything, because a long time ago, we made a pact to never let shit, money or bitches, come between off friendship. That pact was made when we were younger, in elementary school to be exact, and it had stuck with us thus far.

"Aye, the damn money is overflowing. I know we don't suppose to count for another two days, but we got to go ahead and take care of that shit today. Like, asap, my nigga."

"Damn." I groaned, as my dick grew harder.

As many times as my dick hardened from the sound of money, right now it was standing because of my girl. I had Alonso in one ear talking about all the dollars we'd made in a week, and my shawty in the other ear whispering how far she wanted me to stick my dick in her pussy. Shawty said she wanted to feel it in her chest, and I wanted to make her wish come true.

"You need me right now, right now?" I questioned Alonso, hoping that nigga would say no. As the words left my mouth, Chyna turned my head to face her as she started kissing and sucking on my bottom lip. Had she kept on with that shit, Alonso would damn sure be hearing me moan like a bitch. That's how turned on I was right now.

"Yeah... I'm about two minutes away from my house. I already got the money and everything, so you can just meet me there."

"Shit... Aight. I'm about to leave the house now." With that, I ended the call. I took a few minutes to kiss Chyna, and even stood up, with her still straddling me. I laid her down on the bed so that I was now hovering over her. "We gotta make this shit quick," I let her know.

"Quick?" The frown on Chyna's face let me know that she wasn't going for that. "Nah, Papi, this ain't no hit it and leave session. I wanna be held afterwards."

"What? Man, stop playing," I tried leaning down to kiss her lips, but she moved her head. "I can hold you when I get back. It won't be long. Like, three or four hours, tops."

"No, Clarence. I wanna be fucked for like three or four hours, and then cuddle afterwards." She wrapped her arms and legs around me, pulling my face to hers. She started giving me pecks as she said in between them. "You can't stay here with me? Please."

"I can't shawty. I need to go take care of some shit with Lonso. This can't wait. It's important."

"Me getting some of my dick is important! Just tell him to find somebody else to help him. I'm horny."

Shit, I am, too. I wanted to tell her. My dick was so hard that it was hurting, and I knew Shawty dead ass wasn't about to let me fuck her and then leave right now. Yeah, I got away with doing it sometimes, but I knew right now wasn't one of those times.

"Shawty, dead ass, I have to go take care of this. Just let me get a lil' quickie right now, and then when I come back, I give you however many hours you want."

Chyna pressed her lips together as her eyes rolled. My shawty wasn't going for no damn quickie, she wanted the whole fucking thing.

With much attitude laced in her voice, she told me, "I guess I'll just wait until you get back. But if it's late and I'm sleep, you might as well don't even wake me up, because I'ma have a whole ass attitude."

I chuckled as she pushed me off her. I wanted to protest because I needed to release this nut I had building up, but I didn't. I wasn't going to even waste my breath begging for some pussy that I knew would be here when I got back. Plus, I knew she wasn't going to give in to me anyways. My lil' shawty was a feisty little thing, and I liked that shit.

After leaving home, I drove the short distance to the house Alonso had in the hood. Since he got the condo, we mostly did the counting there, so I didn't know why he wanted to meet up here. But I asked as soon as I used my key to let myself inside. He was walking from the back room, drying his hands on a towel. "What's up, nigga? What made you want to meet up here instead of the condo?"

"Man, I didn't even feel like fighting traffic back to the condo. It's a wreck on 285 and it's a two-hour delay. Don't nobody have time for that shit."

I chuckled as I took a seat, glad he didn't make that trip there, because I damn sure didn't want to be stuck in traffic.

"Yeah, I feel you on that." Grabbing one of the duffle bags that I knew consisted of money, I opened it and grabbed a handful of the bills. Me and my nigga was getting to the money and had been that way since a year after we were introduced to the drug world, by Alonso's uncle. He taught us everything we knew, and when he died of a heart attack, we were damn near millionaires, and that was three years ago. So, imagine how much we'd brought in over the years.

Yeah, we were fucking paid at the age of twenty-five.

"Plus, I knew if I would've gone there, I would've been staying there tonight, and I got some business to handle once we take care of this shit."

In response, I nodded.

As we counted the money, we smoked and sipped on some Hennessey. We were halfway done when I thought about Chyna and what she had witnessed today. I couldn't let the day pass without telling Alonso what was up.

I started by saying, "Aye, bruh. We can't sell to Henry's ass no more. Chyna ass rode by and saw him at my car. I tried kicking it to her like I wasn't selling that nigga shit." I chuckled, thinking about how ridiculous that was. I mean, why else he would've been at my car if I weren't selling drugs to his ass? "But anyways, she asked me not to sell to him and I told her I wouldn't."

This time, Alonso chuckled, and shook his head. "I don't see why you still out there slanging dope like you a corner boy anyways. That's what we pay mothafuckas to do."

"Because this shit is what I know, and ain't shit gon' change because I'm sitting on money. I don't give a fuck how much money I got, ain't shit wrong with getting your hands dirty from time to time."

"Yeah, from time to time, but not every damn time." Alonso stopped what he was doing to look at me. "And I can see if this shit was big plays, but yo' ass risking yo' freedom for twenty or thirty damn dollars."

Even I had to laugh when he said that, because the shit was true. It was so fucking true that I didn't even say shit back. I mean, I could argue with the nigga all damn day about my decision, but the facts would still remain the same, he was telling the truth—I was risking my freedom for some damn chump change. But this was the shit I was accustom to. I had been doing it for a long ass time, so it was just a habit for me.

"And, we run this fucking city. So even if you don't sell to him, you'll still get the money for it."

"Oh, I know that, but she don't know." I grinned. "I told her ass, though, if he don't get it from me, he'll get it from someone else. Like, she wants that nigga to get clean, but that nigga ain't going to do that shit. Not no time soon, because he don't feel he have a problem."

"Yeah, you gotta want that change for yourself."

"That's what I told her." I shrugged. "And, why her ass talking about some I ain't shit like my homeboy. Talking about all we do is lie and cheat." When Alonso didn't say shit, I looked up from the money machine I was using to see him putting more bills in his. All the while, he had a look of guilt written on his face. It caused my eyebrow to rise. "Say, nigga, you been cheating on lil' shawty?" I asked, not knowing the shit was true.

Alonso didn't say anything right away, and the nigga didn't have to in order for me to know the truth. It was written on his face. I wasn't even surprised by it. I mean, shawty was a virgin. Don't get me wrong, there wasn't a damn thing wrong with that, but Alonso was a grown ass man. A man with a child already. A man that had many bitches ready to give up the pussy at any time of day to him. He wasn't about to be with someone that had a tight ass grip on their V-card. At least I didn't think he was.

"Damn, bruh, you got my girl calling my ass a cheater for some shit that you did," I laughed out. At first, I was pissed that Chyna tried comparing me to some other nigga, but now I found it comical.

"Man, they run their fucking mouths too damn much. I'ma curse La-La's ass out for telling my gotdamn business." I laughed at the reason he was pissed right now. "And Nicole's ass... I'm going straight to her house to put my foot in her ass."

"Nicole?" I damn near shouted, praying that wasn't who he cheated on Eliza with. That bitch was crazy as fuck. Whether she and Alonso were together or not, she didn't want him fucking with nobody else. Yeah, it was understandable when they were together, but when they weren't, it was a fair game. And don't let my boy call himself moving on from her after one of their many breakups. That bitch would do any and everything until she'd succeeded in running off the bitch that thought she was about to have Alonso to herself.

"Man, it was a slip up. A slip up that I fucking regret." He mumbled the last part. "Then check this... my dumb ass fell asleep there and the bitch got my phone and sent La-La a gotdamn picture of me in her bed, knocked the fuck out."

"Word?" Now I was surprised. My nigga wasn't supposed to had gotten caught slipping like that. He wasn't new to this cheating shit. Whether it was someone you thought you trusted or not, if you had a girl already, you didn't sleep over at the mothafucka's house you were cheating on her with. "And the dumbest nigga award goes to..."

Alonso chuckled, not even taking what I'd just said to the heart. In fact, he co-signed with, "And I'll gladly take that mothafucka, too, because what I did was by far the dumbest shit I'd ever done."

All I could do was laugh and shake my head.

We finished counting money and instead of me heading back home to my girl and Alonso heading to handle whatever business he was planning on handling, we decided to kick it in his front yard, drinking and smoking and eventually a small crowd gathered over. I was sitting on the hood of my car about fucked up off the many blunt I'd smoked and the Henny I was sipping on, when Selena walked over to me. Selena was a chick I used to fuck with before Chyna came along. Shawty was a sexy ass chocolate thing, and if she didn't have four kids at her young ass age, I probably would've made her mine, but I wasn't trying to play daddy to that many kids.

One or two I could handle, but not four. And shawty wasn't nothing but twenty-three. She had her first one when she was only fifteen.

Don't get shit twisted, there was nothing wrong with having kids, but she had four different baby daddies. That was a bit too much for me.

"What's up, boo?" Selena walked in between my legs, grinning from ear to ear, thinking she still had some kind of effect on a nigga.

"Ain't shit. What's up with you, girl?"

"Nothing, just trying to see when you gonna stop playing games and shit with me. It's been months since I last got some dick from you, Clar. What's up with that?"

I chuckled. Selena knew I had a girl and wasn't fucking with her like that no more, but she just refused to accept the fact. "Shawty, you already know the deal. Damn, Kwan ain't enough fo' yo' ass?"

"Fuck Kwan!" Kwan was the nigga she started fucking with after me. Hell, she was probably fucking with him when we were fucking around. It wasn't no telling with her. Selena had been known to fuck with this nigga and that nigga. Word on the streets, she didn't know who her last two kids daddy was—I just knew neither of them were mine. So, I never questioned her on whether it was true or not. Leaning over to me, she pressed her titties against my chest as she whispered in my ear, "Kwan ain't you, and he damn sure don't lay it down like you. I want some real dick."

I laughed as my tongue ran across my lips. "You know I got a girl, right?"

"You talking about that lil' young ass girl?" Her face frowned in disgust. "She's a hoe, but I guess you like that, though, huh?"

I licked my lips. I was about drunk as hell, and about tempted to knock Selena's fucking head off for running her damn mouth so much.

I didn't know why she felt the need to call Chyna a hoe, but I wasn't trying to find out. Figuring it was because Chyna was getting the dick now, and not her, I told her funky ass, "Yeah, I guess I do have a thing for hoes. I mean, I was fucking with you at one point, and everybody knows you one of the biggest hoe in Atlanta. Now gone and get the fuck out my face, shawty."

"No, the biggest hoe of Atlanta would be the bitch that goes around letting niggas run a train on her, and clearly, that's not me."

My eyes narrowed when she said that bullshit. I cocked my head to the side as I fought the urge of asking her what in the fuck she was talking about. I knew a lot of mothafuckas, and a lot of mothafuckas knew Chyna was my girl but not once had I heard anything about her getting a gotdamn train ran on her. The streets talked, and if what Selena's hating ass was saying was true, I would've found out when it first got out that I was fucking with lil' shawty.

Not bothering to feed into Selena's bullshit, I simply said, "Might as well. You don't even know who your gotdamn baby daddy is."

When I threw that in her face, she tried reaching up to slap me, but she was too gotdamn slow. I grabbed her wrist and twisted it as I hopped off my car. The few people in the yard were looking over at us but dared to not come interfere. When I was off my car, I turned her around so that she was facing me. Pushing her upper body backward, onto my car, I leaned down, getting all in her face. I was so close in her face that I knew for a fact that my lips were about to brush against hers once I spoke, but I didn't give a fuck.

"Clarence, you're hurting my arm. Get off me."

"Shut the fuck up!" I told her. "Call my girl a hoe again... Nah, fuck that. Say one more thing about my shawty, and I'ma rock you in yo' shit, and I'm not only talking about tonight. If I hear or it get back to me that me and my girl's name been in yo' shit, I'm fucking your ass up, Selena. Now try me if you want to."

"Aye, bruh... Chill out." I felt Alonso tap my shoulder as he said that. A lot of people were out, and the last thing he or me needed was for someone to call the police on my black ass, or for me to incriminate myself by threatening her. "Let her ass go so she can get the fuck up out my damn yard."

I didn't let her go right away and even applied a little more pressure to her wrist before I let her ass go. When I did, she didn't say shit as she took off, hurriedly walking out the yard. Her flunkies had to damn near run to catch up with her.

"Aye, all ya'll asses get the fuck up out my gotdamn yard. That bitch done fucked it up for all ya'll mothafuckas." Alonso didn't have to tell them to leave a second time as they bolted out his front yard. "You good, bruh?" He asked me.

"Yeah. I'm going to end up killing that dumb ass hoe."

Alonso chuckled. "Nah, I think she got the picture. Her ass ain't that fucking crazy to keep speaking on lil' shawty after you done threatened to fuck her up." He just didn't know Selena like I knew her. "But check this. Help me bring the bags to my car. I'ma go ahead and stay at the condo tonight. I don't wanna stay here with all this damn money."

We had made over a hundred thousand in two weeks, and I felt where Alonso was coming from by not wanting to stay in the hood with that amount of cash.

After we got the money up, I headed home to my shawty. When I got there, she was knocked out. I didn't bother taking off my clothes as I walked over to her side of the bed and hovered over her. She tried to front like she didn't want me waking her up, but I knew she was just talking shit. Chyna loved when I woke her ass up.

"Bae," I whispered, causing her to stir but not open her eyes. "Turn over, Chy." She was on her side, but I needed her on her damn back.

"What I tell you, Clarence? I knew you wasn't coming right back." Leaning down, I started trailing my kisses from her shoulder to her back. It wasn't long before she turned over and that's when her eyes popped open. Chyna pushed me away as she hurriedly sat up. Grabbing my shirt, she pulled me down to her and started sniffing me.

"What the fuck is wrong with you?" I asked in confusion.

"Why the fuck do you smell like a bitch?" I sucked my teeth and walked off. I smelled Selena's perfume when she was all over me, but I didn't think the shit would linger on my clothes or nothing like that. It was a bad look, especially when Alonso had just gotten caught up cheating and my girl was now questioning my ass. "Don't walk off from me. What bitch you been with?"

She was out of the bed and now into my closet with me as I removed my clothes. "I haven't been with no bitch. I was at Alonso's house."

"Well, what the fuck ya'll been doing? Is there something La-La and me need to know?"

I turned around to look at her so fast when she said that. "Aye, don't get fucked up!"

"I'm just saying. You clearly smell like a woman, and you say you wasn't—"

I cut her off.

"Look, we were outside kicking it and it was bitches over there, but I wasn't fucking with none of their asses." I told her, truthfully.

"Here comes the bullshit." Chyna threw her hands in the air, dramatically, as she turned around. "I don't know what the fuck Alonso and La-La got going on, but I'm not about to be with a cheater. I know I'm young and everything, but if this ain't what you want, then tell me so I can get the fuck—"

I walked over to the bed where she was getting back underneath the covers and yanked it off her. Grabbing her hand, I pulled her out the bed and picked her up bridal style. "Try to leave me if yo' ass want to. I swear to God, you don't want to see that side of me."

"Well, don't give me a reason to, Clarence. You don't come back in a couple of hours like you promised and then when you do come, you smell like a whole bitch. I don't like that." She frowned and rolled her eyes.

I chuckled as I licked my lips. "Shawty, dead ass... I promise, I wasn't with no other woman. What? You wanna smell my dick or something?"

Her frown hardened. "Hell no. I'm not that type. If I have to smell your dick every time you leave and come back, I don't need to be with you. But what you can do is, take your stinking ass in there and wash that stinking ass, so called perfume off, because it's messing with my allergies."

I chuckled as I kissed her lips and damn near threw her back on the bed. I didn't bother telling Chyna why I smelled like another woman, because then I would've had to tell her what all was said.

A part of me wanted to know about that damn train Selena was referring to, but the other part wanted to believe she was talking out the side of her fucking neck because she was a jealous ass hoe, and if it was true, I had no reason to believe it happened since me and Chyna had been together. Yet and still, I didn't know if I wanted to be with somebody that went around fucking multiple niggas at a time. That wasn't my style, and if Chyna had done some hoe shit like that, I needed to reevaluate this fucking relationship with her, but how could I reconsider a relationship that I was putting my all into?

I was doing shit for shawty that I had never done for no other bitch. Letting her drive my car, stay with me... I didn't do none of that bullshit. This was a first, and I wasn't going to even front, hearing Selena say that bullshit fucked a nigga all the way up.

II

Alonso Davis

*a*fter leaving my house, I drove straight home, to my condo. I had the mindset to go by Nicole's place to put my foot in her ass, but I quickly changed my mind when I got in the car. I was drunk and high and didn't have no business going over there. Not because I was scared that I would sleep with her again, but because I was afraid of what I would do to her once my eyes landed on her.

Now, it was a new morning and before I did anything else after leaving this condo, I was paying her funky ass a visit. First thing first, I had to text Eliza to make sure she was straight. I didn't talk to her none the day before because I was waiting on her to call me, but surprisedly, she didn't. So, this morning, I was calling her. I was sure to wake up extra early to hit her up, and I wasn't talking about the text I sent every morning. I was calling because I knew she wasn't in class yet.

"Hey?" Eliza answered in a whisper.

"What's up, lil' mama? You good?" I asked. She hit me with a, *Mmhmm,* and I frowned. I was familiar with that shit because she did it when she was upset and didn't want to be bothered. Still, I told her, "I'm coming to pick you up from school."

"Alonso, I have to go straight home from school. I can't be out messing around."

"Shawty, I'll have you home." My tone was a little louder than I intended on it to be, and my voice was filled with frustration. "And when the fuck you start calling being with me messing around? Are you still mad about something that I already apologized for?"

"Just because you apologized doesn't make it all better, Lonso."

"So what you saying, you don't forgive me?" I knew my apology didn't make anything better or change the fact that I cheated on her, but I wanted her to know that I meant the shit from the heart. I wanted my lil' mama to forgive me. I needed for Eliza to allow a nigga to make it up to her, and I was willing to do anything, because I didn't want to lose her. "Huh? Is that what you're saying?"

I heard her release a deep breath before she finally spoke up. She said, "I don't know, Alonso." She paused and mumbled something that I didn't understand. Before I could ask her what she had just said, she told me. "Look, the bell is about to ring, and I need to get to class. I'm not going to my last class, so if you planning on coming to get me, then you need to be here around 2:15."

After telling her that I would be there, I said I love you, but I didn't even think shawty heard me with how fast she hung up in my damn face. All I could do was shake my fucking head as I took the phone from my ear. I rubbed my hand down my face as I stared out the large window, thinking about how bad I had fucked up, and Eliza wasn't the type to just brush this shit off, I could tell. But, as I stated before, I was willing to go the extreme to show her that Nicole's ass didn't mean shit to me. The only thing that trifling bitch was to me, was the mother of my son, and that alone.

When I finally left my condo, I made a stop at Tiffany jewelry to pick up something for Eliza. I knew it still wouldn't change what I'd done, but I prayed it was a start. That fucking girl was my world, and I wanted her to know nothing I did would ever change that. Dead ass!

After leaving Tiffany's, I only had one hour to spare before I headed to Eliza school to pick her up. Since Nicole didn't live too far from her school, I stopped by her house first. Her front door was open, so I knew she was home. I parked in front of the house and got out.

"What do you want, Lonso? You haven't called or anything to check on your son," Nicole spat when she walked up to the screen door. I knew it was locked because I tried opening it when I first walked up to it.

"Open the fucking door!"

"Nope. You ain't running shit, and AJ is at school—which, I doubt you came over to see him." The smile displayed on her face let me know that this bitch knew I was here to fuck her ass up. Nicole was an evil, bitter ass bitch, and every fucking day I was starting to hate her ass more. "I guess your lil' ass girlfriend told you she got the picture."

"You trifling as fuck, bitch. Why the fuck would yo' dumb ass do some bogus ass shit like that? That's why I don't fuck with you now."

"I'm trifling? Nigga, you the trifling one. How the fuck you mad at me because you cheated on your bitch? When will you learn, Lonso? I don't play no fucking games when it comes to you, boo. Any bitch that think she is about to live a happy life with you is sadly mistaken. When I got pregnant with AJ, you told me we were in this thing forever, and I be damn if some little young ass bitch that barely knows how to wipe her ass good, is going to take you from me." Nicole shouted. The conniving grin that she once wore on her face had vanished, and she now held a serious expression.

"Listen, I don't give a fuck what promise I made to you back then, that shit is dead and gone, shawty. You know I don't have no fucking feelings for yo' ass no more, why the fuck you can't just move on. I know you got niggas that you're fucking with now, be happy with them."

"No... I'ma be happy with the nigga that promised to love me forever. Ya'll mothafuckas think ya'll can just play with a bitch's heart and everything supposed to be all good. Hell the fuck no! It don't work like that, and if you and Miss. Young Thang think ya'll about to be happy—"

"Why the fuck you so bitter? You keep calling my girl young and shit, but her young ass got you pressed like a mothafucka." I cut her ass off because I didn't know how much more of her threat I could take. Nicole was really pushing me to a limit I didn't want to be on. She was the mother of my kids, and Lord knows I didn't want to bodily harm her, but had she kept on with her B.S, that's exactly what was going to happen.

"Fuck her, Lonso. We'll see who comes off on top. You know how I get down. How many other bitches have you tried moving on with?" When she asked that, I narrowed my eyes. "Exactly. Nigga, you always end back up here, where you belong. Either you end that shit, or I will do it for you."

Just as the words left her mouth, I hauled back and punched the shit out of her glass door, shattering it. Nicole jumped back and yelled. I took a step towards the door but stopped. I knew had I gone inside that house I would've beat her ass, or even worse, killed her. I wasn't at all a woman beater, but Nicole had a way of pushing my buttons. In a way, I think it turned her on, but right now, I wasn't even about to give her the satisfaction. So, I quietly turned around and headed back to my car, ignoring her yelling and cursing my ass out about her damn door.

When I got inside my car, I saw my hand was bleeding. It wasn't much, but it was there.

"Damn," I mumbled as I pulled off.

When I got at the stop sign down the street from Nicole's house, I hopped out and looked in my trunk for a shirt. Luckily, I kept clothes and shit in my car. When I got back inside, I wrapped a white tank top around my hand and headed to Eliza's school to pick her up. At 2:15, my shawty was walking out to my car. Seeing her caused me to smile, as well as my heart to ache.

"What's up, bae?" I said as I pulled off. She mouthed the word, hey, back and I shook my head.

"What happened to your hand?" I looked over to see that she was eyeing the shirt that was wrapped around it. When I followed her eyes, I saw the little blood that had seethe through.

"Oh, I fucked around and cut myself on some broken glass." She asked to see, and I stretch my hand out for her to unwrap it. It looked pretty bad, but it wasn't bad enough to go to the hospital or anything like that.

"You need to stop at the store to get some alcohol or peroxide. Trust, you do not want that shit to get infected." It was a dollar store coming up and I pulled up in there. To avoid anyone seeing her, I told her I would go inside to get it. When I came back out, Eliza got my hand together right in the parking lot. I watched her as she tended to my hand. She was just so fucking beautiful, and I loved every fucking thing about her. I just hated she had to be so damn young.

Breaking the silence, I told her, "You know I really am sorry about what I did, La-La, and I want you to forgive me."

For a minute, she just sat there and didn't say a word. When she did, she couldn't even look at a nigga. "You hurt me, Alonso. This girl already hates me and refers to you as, *her nigga*, then you go out and cheat with her. It makes me think it's been going on all this time."

"But it haven't. I already told you that, and you don't have to worry about the shit happening again. I put that on my son's life."

"No!" Eliza held up her index finger in my face. "I will not let you put shit like that on that baby's life."

"But I mean it." I licked my lips as I grabbed her hand and started placing kisses on it. Between the kisses, I told her, "She don't mean shit to me. You do. You're the one I wanna be with."

"Why?" I jerked my head back and looked at her through a confused grimace, wondering what the fuck she meant, why. It was like she read my mind, too. "I mean, why you wanna be with me. Look at me."

"I'm looking…"

"I'm seventeen. I can't even stay out pass twelve o'clock. I was a virgin when we met, Alonso. A virgin… I even lied to you and told you I was eighteen, only for my mama to call and tell you the truth." By now, Eliza had tears leaking from her eyes. "Why would you want to be with someone like me? Judging from your baby mama, I'm nowhere near your type. My body isn't filled out like hers. We look different. We're just the total opposite."

She was right. Every fucking thing Eliza was saying was true, and

I wasn't going to even sit here and pretend that I haven't asked myself why her over the other women that were lined up to be with me, because I have. But the truth was, I didn't give a fuck about none of that. Yeah, it pissed me off and frustrated me that she couldn't stay the night with me, or I couldn't fuck her like I wanted to, due to me not being ready to take her virginity. Hell, I didn't even think she was ready, but instead, she portrayed herself to be because her homegirls were having sex.

And when it came to Nicole and her being opposite, they were in many ways. Nicole was a hoodrat, and once upon of time, I loved that shit. As I got older, I wanted more. No, I didn't at all think I would find what I was looking for in someone much younger, but I did, and now, I wasn't trying to lose her.

"I don't give a fuck about none of that. Patience is the key, and when it comes to you, I have all the patience in the world. You know why?" I asked but didn't give her a chance to answer. "Because I fucking love you. Yeah, the situation is aggravating as fuck, but I'm too deep in. I'm too fucking in love to just walk away now. That's why I couldn't do the shit when mom dukes told me your real age. I tried. I mean, I wanted to like a mothafucka, but... but that shit just ain't gon' happen. And as far as you and Nicole, if I wanted somebody that would remind me of her, then I would still be with her."

Eliza dropped her head as she eased her hand away from me. She started fidgeting with her nails and I took it as an opportunity to give her the gift I had gotten for her.

"Here. I got you something."

"What is it?"

"Open it and see."

Taking the box from me, she opened the small black velvet box and her mouth fell open. She looked at me through her bucked eyes. "Alonso... I—I can't marry you."

I chuckled when she said that as I took the box out her hand. Removing the 1.5 oval shaped diamond ring from the box, I grabbed her right hand and placed it on her ring finger. It was a perfect fit. "Your engagement ring will be much bigger than this shit. This is a promise ring. It's my promise to never hurt you or give you a reason to question my love for you. I love the fuck out of you, Eliza, and I can't stress that shit enough. I swear, you just don't know what all I got in stores for us."

"Awww. Bae, I love you, too." Eliza admitted as she looked up from the ring to me. She mustered up a smile. "I don't want to lose you either, but... but I do need some time to think about all this. I mean, everything is still fresh, and... I just... I just don't want to be made a fool of. You mean so much to me, but we both need to see if this is what we really want."

I frowned as I leaned away from her, propping up on my door. "You mean you need to see if this shit is what you really want, huh?" I knew she was what I wanted, so she wasn't speaking about me when she said that bullshit. She dropped her head, unable to look at my ass, and her behavior caused me to chuckle. "Shawty, you don't have to try and protect me. Say what the fuck it is on your mind."

Her tongue ran across her lips as she looked over at me. Eliza looked me dead in the mothafuckin' eyes and told me, "I don't know if I can still trust you. I told you so many times, before you cheat on me, just leave me. And not only did you cheat and do it with the one bitch that doesn't like me, but you allowed her to take a picture and send it to me."

"Hold the fuck up. I didn't allow her ass to do a gotdamn thing."

"Yes you did. When you went to sleep, you allowed it." I didn't say shit. I mean, what in the hell could I really say to that? "So, no. I don't know if I could trust you."

She started motioning like she was going to take the ring off, but I grabbed her hand, preventing her from doing that. With a shake of my head, I told her, "Nah. Go ahead and keep that. I gave it to you. It's yours." I paused to lick my lips and run my hands down my face and over my full beard. "I love you, Eliza, and I can never say that shit enough. I told myself that I was willing to do anything to get you to forgive me, and I meant that shit. As bad as I hate to say it, if giving you time to figure out if this is what you want or not is what you need, I can respect that." With that, I started my car. As I threw it in reverse and back out the parking space, I heard her mumble, *thank you*.

I wasn't going to even lie, a nigga was pissed beyond fucking words. Yet, I kept my cool. I mean, she was young. She had her whole life ahead of her, and if she didn't want to be with my ass because of my fuck up, I didn't have no other choice but to accept that.

12

Eliza Brown

On the ride to drop me off, neither, Alonso nor me said a word. My eyes roamed the car, looking straight ahead, down at my ring and to the left of me, at Alonso. He didn't look at me at all. He was wearing an unreadable expression as he kept his eyes fixed on the road ahead. I wanted to ask what was on his mind, but I thought against it. I was afraid of what he'd say.

I loved Alonso, and that went without saying, but I wasn't about to give him the pleasure of thinking he would walk all over my heart. Bad enough I had given him my innocence the day after he cheated. I was hurt, and as crazy as it might sound, I thought if we consummated our relationship that day, it would've been easier for me to forgive him. I was wrong. In fact, it made it a lot harder. Most of all, it made me feel like a fucking fool. And for that reason alone, I had yet to tell my girls about it.

"Do you want me to call you later on, or—"

Still unable to look at me, he said, "Shawty, it don't even matter. If you call, you call, if you don't, you don't."

I frowned as my head jerked back to look at this nigga like he had lost his fucking mind. "Really, Alonso? So, it's like that?"

"Man, look, you say you need some time, right?" He looked over at me when he asked that, causing me to narrow my eyes at his ass. "I'm willing to give you the time you need. So, if you call me, it doesn't matter, but if I call you that mean I'm not giving you the time you want. Right?"

He had a good ass point, but still... He didn't have to be so gotdamn nonchalant about it. With a roll of my eyes, I said a stiff, *whatever*, and gathered my stuff to get out. When I opened the door, I threw one leg out and said, "Thanks for the ride."

In response, Alonso nodded his head up and down and I closed the door. I didn't understand why it appeared he had an attitude all because I said I needed some time. I was pretty sure if I had been the one that cheated, his reaction would've been a whole lot different. As I unlocked my front door, my phone vibrated in my back pocket. When I looked at it, it was a text from Alonso that read, *don't keep me waiting too long.*

My lips twisted from side to side as I tried holding my smile in, but completely fail. After doing my homework, I decided to take a nap. I knew I had been asleep for a few hours because my mama was home and standing on the side of my bed, calling my name.

"Hmmm?" I scrunched my face up as I batted my eyes a few times, trying to adjust them to the light.

"Um, Zola and Chyna outside for you." With that, my mama turned around and walked off.

Reaching over, I grabbed my phone to check the time. It was 6:46 p.m. *Damn.* I couldn't believe I had slept for that long. I dragged myself out of bed and went right into the bathroom to use it and make sure I was up to par before I went outside where my girls were.

"Dang, girl, I thought something had happened to you. Why haven't you been answering the phone for us?" Chyna fussed the minute I stepped on the porch.

Even Zola added her two cents by saying, "Exactly. You had us worried."

"Worried, why? Ya'll know I'm on punishment. I can't go nowhere so why not sleep the day away."

"Hell, nawl... Fuck the punishment. What in the hell is this, La-

La? Did that nigga propose to you?" That quick, Chyna had spotted my ring. She grabbed my hand and snatched it over to examine it. "And this shit is huge. Girl, Mrs. Erika is going to beat your—"

Zola snatched my hand to look for herself. "What the hell, La-La? Didn't this nigga just cheat on you?"

"Will ya'll hoes be quiet... Damn!" I snatched my hand from Zola's grasp and looked back at my front door to make sure my mama wasn't eavesdropping. "And this is not no damn engagement ring. It's a promise ring."

"A promise ring? That damn big?" Chyna grabbed my hand to look at the ring again. "This shit is huge, and nice as fuck."

"Well, he is a little too late to be giving you a damn promise ring." Zola rolled her eyes. "He should've given you that before he cheated, not afterwards."

I pressed my lips together as I looked over at Chyna. She was eyeing Zola through a frowned as she said, "Zola, chill the hell out. It is not that deep, boo."

"Exactly..." I added.

"I'm just saying... He's trying to give her a funky little ring to make up for what he did. What he do, feed you a bunch of lies on how he's sorry and he'll never do it again?" Zola's eyes rolled. "Girl, please. It's a good thing you didn't give that nigga sex because then you would've lost your v-card to an ain't shit ass nigga—which, all these niggas are the same in my opinion."

"Nope. Hell, no. Not my Clarence." Chyna rolled her eyes. "You speak about your nigga. My boo ain't like the rest of these niggas."

"And how the hell you know? I heard him and Alonso had plenty of bitches at Alonso's house the other night." My eyebrows shot up when Zola threw that out there. I was just about to ask her when was this and what happened when those bitches were at Alonso's house, but I didn't get a chance because she continued looking at Chyna, rolling her neck as she added, "And, *your boo*, had some bitch in between his legs and shit."

"What? Bitch, stop capping." Chyna shot back. "I know he was at Alonso's house and mothafuckas was over there, but I seriously doubt Clarence would've been that bold. You want everybody's relationship to be fucked up so it can look like you have the perfect nigga. Girl, get the fuck out of here."

"Alright, ya'll. Chill the hell out before my mom come out here." I told them. The last thing I wanted or needed was for my mama to come out and see this big ass ring on my finger. No, it wasn't on my left hand, but still, she would question me as if it was. Turning to look at Zola, I asked, "Now what in the hell is you talking about Zola. What girls were at Alonso's house?"

Yes, we were going through something at the moment, but that didn't mean I didn't want to know what bitch he had at his house. *See?* This shit right here made me happy for telling him that I needed some time to think about if I wanted to be with his ass or not. Alonso was slowly showing me a side of him that I wasn't sure I liked.

"La-La, you better not believe Zola's ass. She's just trying to make us think it was more than it was." Chyna turned her attention back to Zola. "What is your problem, Zola? Why you trying to fill her head up with a bunch of bullshit? This girl is already going through enough, and now you got her thinking the nigga is—"

"Partying and having a ball while she is home crying her eyes out?" Zola snapped. "I'm not trying to make her think anything, Chy. I'm just letting you and her know what ya'll niggas is up to when ya'll not around."

"And what is Prince doing when you're not around?"

Zola chuckled at Chyna's question. "Oh, that's one thing I'm not worried about. He knows he don't have a reason to cheat on me." A wide smile grew on her face when she expressed that, causing me to frown because I felt like she was throwing jabs at me. I was the virgin that had gotten cheated on. So, it was only right her little statement offended me.

"And what the hell does that supposed to mean, Zola?"

"Yeah, Zola." Chyna spoke up in my defense. "What does that supposed to mean?"

"Just what I said, he doesn't have a reason to cheat on me."

While I just glared at her, Chyna was ready to go toe to toe with her ass, and I knew neither of them would back down to the other. "You just said all niggas ain't shit. So, what in the fuck make Prince so different?"

"Because maybe he is..." Zola had a smug look on her face.

While I just wanted to change the subject at this point, Chyna wanted to keep going back and forth with the damn girl. Just like me, she knew how Zola was. She wanted to be the mama of the group and tell us how to handle *our* relationship. Chyna swore Zola didn't want anyone to be happy but her, and judging from her behavior today, I was starting to agree.

"Zola, you full of shit." Chyna waved her off. "Anyway, La-La. So, are you going to forgive Lonso, or move on?"

"I don't know, yet." I shrugged as I looked down at the promise ring he'd given me. "I want to, but I don't want to be so quick to do so. Like, I don't want him to think he can keep pulling this shit."

"Exactly, remember what I said, once you let these mothafucka slide, they start trying to ice skate," said Chyna. "I'm not saying you should or shouldn't forgive him, but if you do, make sure that nigga know he better not pull that shit again."

"I just want one sign from God." I looked up at the sky as if I was talking to God himself. "God, please, just give me one sign on why I shouldn't take this nigga back." My voice was in a jokingly manner, but hey, I was dead ass serious. "Just one. That's all I ask."

Chyna and Zola laughed at my antics.

The rest of their stay, we talked about nothing in particular. I was just happy that my relationship with Alonso was no longer the hot topic.

After my girls had left, I went back inside to my mama sitting on the couch, watching TV and smoking her cigarette. I was in the kitchen fixing me something to eat when she walked in to fix her a second plate. Remembering I still had on the ring, I tried slipping it off my finger and stuffing it into my front pocket before she could see it.

I thought I had succeeded until she said, "You don't have to hide that from me. I saw the damn thing when I walked in your room to wake you up."

I dropped my head, preparing myself for the cursing out that I knew was bound to come. When it didn't, I told her, "It's not an engagement ring. It's a promise ring. You know, just a gift."

"I don't even give a damn, La-La, because you think you grown and you gonna do what you wanna do. Let me tell you this, though. That's a grown ass man, and while you trying to play grown like you ready for him, you better be ready for the bullshit that comes along with his ass." With that said, my mama turned around and walked out the kitchen without giving me another look. Her word stung, and it was almost as if she knew something.

I wanted to ask, but I was too afraid to. Too embarrassed. If the bullshit that came with Alonso was deeper than him cheating on me, there was no way I was ready for it. *Was this the sign I asked God for?* I wondered as I grabbed my plate and walked out the kitchen. They say mother knows best, and right now, I wondered if that saying was true, or was my mama trying to scare me into leaving him alone.

At this point, it had me asking God for another sign, because right now I was ignoring this one.

I WAS FINALLY OFF PUNISHMENT AND THE FIRST THING I WANTED TO DO was, hang with my girls. I had only talked to Alonso once since I told him that I needed some time, and when I did talk to him, he was dry with me after I told him that I didn't want him coming to pick me up from school. So that called didn't last long at all. I wasn't worried about it, though. I missed him, but it was whatever.

"Yesssss... My bitch is finally free. I thought you was going to bring in your birthday on punishment, bitch." Chyna said as she threw her arms around my neck, causing me to laugh. I was so happy that she had Clarence car. That way I didn't have to go straight home.

"Don't try to be funny." I shrugged her off me, still laughing. It did feel like I was on that damn punishment forever. But, I was a month away from my eighteenth birthday and I knew I was going to be off way before then. "So, where we about to go? I been in the house for too long and I'm not trying to go straight home."

"I bet you not." Chyna laughed out as we got inside the car. "I guess we can go to Clarence's house and chill. And girl, why I been in a good mood all freakin' day. Like, it just hit me. Can you believe we're actually about to graduate?"

Her saying that caused a huge smile to grow on my face. I was walking down the aisle to get my high school diploma one week after my eighteenth birthday. My girl and I had actually did it. Zola had done it a year before us, and now it was our turn. I swear, the turn up is going to be real. And you know how I knew it was going to be out of this world? Because we had already booked our flight and room in Jamaica. I couldn't wait.

"I'm just ready for that trip. Child, I'ma be like a new person."

"I know that's right." Chyna started popping her coochie in her seat. I even threw my hands in the air and did the same. On the real, I couldn't believe my mama was even letting me go. While I often said she was so strict on my ass, I knew she was only looking out for me. "I don't know what the hell Clarence going to do while I'm gone, but I know what he better not do, and that's entertain these hoes. That nigga don't know it, but I'm going to have eyes on his ass. You want me to get somebody to watch over your nigga, too?"

"Girl, no!" I frowned as I jerked my head to look at her. "Did you forget? Me and Alonso ain't together no more."

"So ya'll not going to get back together by then?" I shrugged as I pressed my lips together. "Damn. I know I told you to not be so quick to forgive him, but dang... I didn't know you was going to make the nigga sweat this long."

"Trust, he is not sweating." I rolled my eyes as I looked down at my ring. "I haven't talked to Alonso but once since he gave me this ring. He hasn't called me or anything. So, I seriously doubt he is sweating over me. He might be somewhere kicking it with his baby mama."

"Hmmm"

"Hmmm, what?" I threw my back against the door so I could get a clear view of Chyna, trying to see what in the hell she knew, or heard about Alonso. I was still looking for that sign from God. Other than the shit my mama was spitting, I hadn't received one. "What the hell you know that I don't?"

"Girl, chill out. I don't know anything. That hum means I don't want to get in it, but I like Alonso. Like, he's cool as hell, with his smart ass mouth." I pressed my lips together and sat back up straight. When she noticed I wasn't going to say anything, she changed the subject. "Lets call Zola and see where her hot pussy at. Knowing her, she's probably up under Prince ass."

"You already know she is." We both laughed as she dialed Zola's number. When Zola's voice came through the car radio, I screamed her name. "Zolaaaaaaaa."

"Elizaaaaaa." Me and Zola laughed as I cut my eyes at Chyna. She had sucked her teeth and was playfully rolling her eyes. "It says Chyna. Where she at?"

"It says Chyna because I'm the one that called you, tramp." We all laughed. The little disagreements we always had never last long. "Where you at? We about to come fuck with you."

"I doubt ya'll wanna come fuck with me." She sucked her teeth. "I'm over here at Alonso's house with Prince, but your boo is here, Chyna."

Chyna looked over at me with eagerly eyes. Hearing Clarence was there had my girl ready to press down hard on that accelerator and speed to her man. Me on the other hand, I rolled my eyes and looked out the passenger window. I wasn't ready to see Alonso, but at the same time, I didn't want to go home or stop my girl from seeing her nigga, and I knew shit was probably jumping over there. We all had hung out at Alonso's place plenty of times before, and it was always popping.

"What you wanna do?" Chyna asked me. "You wanna roll up on those fools or what, B?"

I chuckled at her trying to talk like she was from New York.

"It doesn't matter. I just know I'm not ready to go home."

"Bet... We're on the way, trick." With that, Chyna's rude ass ended the call. She was known to hang up in people faces, so that was nothing new. On the way to Alonso's house, we made small talk, mostly with Chyna telling me that we didn't have to go there if I didn't want to, but I assured her that it was fine. I mean, it wasn't like anything would happen that I didn't want to. Despite the shit Alonso did, he had always been respectful to me. So, I wasn't worried about anything.

Even so, the closer we got to his house, the tenser I became. I didn't know what to say to him, or if he would even acknowledge my ass. So much was running through my mind, and Chyna just had to open her mouth and say some dumb mess. She said, "Oh, what if we pull up and that nigga is hugged up with another bitch?"

I looked at Chyna like she was crazy. Right then, I could've smacked the piss out of her for putting that crap in my head. If I wasn't nervous before, I damn sure was now.

"Oh my God, why you sitting there looking like you about to cry. You know that man is not that crazy to do that shit with Zola there." Chyna laughed. That somewhat eased my mind, but you never knew. Pulling up to the house, Alonso was the first person I saw. I didn't know if it was because I was looking for him, or what, but when my eyes landed on him, it caused my breathing to thicken.

Gosh. I really loved this man.

"Now, you know you don't have to say shit to him if you don't want to," Chyna told me before we got out.

"Hey boo, you good?" Zola met us at the car and asked me. I felt like a small child at the moment, but I knew their intentions weren't to make me feel as such. My girls just knew I had never been through anything like this. Hell, Alonso was my first real boyfriend. So this shit we were going through was breaking a bitch.

"Yes." I let out a laugh. "I'm good. Ya'll acting like this nigga is about to beat my ass or something."

"Oh, he knows better. But, girl, I think that nigga is really messed up right now." I frowned as I looked at Zola through questionable eyes. "He hasn't been acting like himself. He just been quiet and shit. He was in the house a long time before he came out."

"Really?" I raised an eyebrow, wondering what that was about. When I turned my head to look back over at Alonso, he was staring directly at me. I immediately dropped my head, knowing damn well he saw me. "Maybe he is going through something. I haven't talked to him in a few days."

Zola just stared at me. I could tell she wanted to say something, and I was glad she didn't. I didn't want to hear anything else about my relationship with Alonso.

"What's up, La-La?" Prince walked to the side of the road where Zola and I were. He wrapped his arms around her neck and kissed her cheek. Those two acted as if they were so in love, and there was nothing wrong with that, but damn... I didn't need them rubbing it in my face. Letting out a chuckle at my ridiculousness, I shook my head as I spoke back. "You wanna hit this blunt?"

"Hell, no." I frowned. "You know I don't smoke. You better pass that shit to your girl." Zola didn't waste no time laughing and taking the blunt from his hand. While they smoked and gave each other shotguns, I walked up to the house. Alonso was still sitting on the car, staring at me. A part of me wanted to run over to him, tell him that I made up my mind and with him is where I wanted to be. However, the stubborn side of me wouldn't allow that to happen. He had fucked up, not me.

"La-La... What's up, shawty?" Clarence spoke as he nudged me. "I see you free from the pen." I sucked my teeth as Chyna and me hit him at the same time. I was so damn embarrassed and prayed the other few people out there didn't know what he was talking about.

"Shut up, Clare. You get on my damn nerves."

"Man, you know I'm just fucking with you." He tried wrapping one arm around my neck in a playful manner, but I pushed him away. Although I was embarrassed, I wasn't really mad forreal. "So, what ya'll got going on?" I asked. I felt awkward, so I just wanted to spark up a conversation. Zola was still onside of the road, smoking and hugged up with Prince, and Clarence and Chyna were attached at the hip. Alonso was still sitting on the freakin' car, staring at me like he wanted to say something but didn't know what.

"Shit, just kicking it. You know this shit is an everyday thing." Clarence was right. Wherever they were, they drew traffic. Hell, if they were posted at his house, it would've been way more people than the few that was out now. Alonso didn't allow that, and when he got tired of folks being in his front yard or standing in front of his house, he would be sure to let them know they had to go.

"That's what's up?" I said with a bob of my head. I then looked over at Alonso. I was sick of his staring, so I asked, "What's up, Alonso?"

This crazy man didn't smile or anything as he said, "You tell me, Eliza."

My eyes narrowed before they rolled without my consent. I pressed my lips as I turned my head away from him. His ass was so damn fine when he was upset. I couldn't even look at him, but I should've known he wasn't going to let me off the hook that easy. Before I knew it, he had gotten off the car and walked up on me.

"Come here, let me talk to you for a minute." He turned around and walked in toward the house, like he just knew I was going to follow him—which, I did. Inside the house, he walked over and took a seat on the couch, after he had closed the front door. I was sure to keep my distance as I asked what was up. "Damn. So you scared to come near me, now?" Alonso frown, looking offended.

Slowly, I walked over and took a seat next to him, but I left a small gap between us.

"Man, how long you gon' keep playing yo' childish ass games?"

"What childish games am I playing, Lonso?"

"You ain't dumb, shawty. You know what the fuck I'm talking about. Stop acting like you don't miss me." I pressed my lips and turned to look straight ahead. Swiftly, Alonso pushed me backwards with his body and hovered over me. He stared me directly in the eyes without saying anything, but the stare ended when the front door opened. I tried to jump up, but due to Alonso taking his sweet little time to get off me, I couldn't.

"You good, La-La?" Zola asked. I looked up to see her and Chyna standing there.

"Fuck you mean is she good? Why wouldn't she be?" Alonso questioned, turning around and scowling at them. I didn't know what in the hell he had against my damn friends, but he always acted as if he had a problem with them or something, like they had done something to him.

When I saw Chyna frown and get ready to retort something, I jumped up and started straightening out my clothes. She and Alonso, both, had smart ass mouths, and I didn't feel like hearing those two go at it. "Yeah, I'm good, ya'll."

"Well, we're about to go to the mall. I can drop you off when we leave there."

"Okay, that's—" I was about to say that was fine and we could leave when Alonso grabbed my hand. He didn't say anything, but the look in his eyes said he wanted me to stay. While a part of me wanted to ignore the look he was giving me, the other part couldn't. I missed this man with a passion. I was longing for him right now, and not just sexually. I wanted us to go back to the way we were. The way we were before his cheating ass decided to cheat on me. "Alonso can drop me off at home."

"Are you sure?" Zola asked and I nodded. I could see the disappointment in her eyes, but I chose to ignore that just as I'd been ignoring a lot of things lately. "Well, we can just to tomorrow or something."

"Yeah, that's cool with me." When they changed their plans, I felt bad. I didn't want them changing their plans because of me, so I told them they could go ahead and go, I'll be fine. One thing I knew about Alonso, he wouldn't do shit to physically harm me. "Nawl, girl. It's cool. None of us have shit to do tomorrow. We can go then."

With a nod of my head, I replied back with, "Okay, ya'll. I'll be out there in a minute." After they gave Alonso a hard look, they finally went back outside, slamming the door behind them. I knew that was Chyna that had done that because she was just that bold.

With a straight face, Alonso looked up at me and said, "Aye, your fucking friends gon' make me fuck them up."

"Whatever. You better leave them alone." I rolled my eyes as he was standing. Grabbing my hand, he started walking toward the back of the house, to his bedroom. I really didn't know why, though, because I wasn't about to have sex with his ass. "What are you doing?" Although I was pulling back, I was still taking steps, following him.

"I just wanna talk. That's it."

"But we were just talking up front, Alonso. If you think we're about to have sex again—" He hushed me with a kiss as soon as we entered his room. As he parted my lips with his tongue and eased it inside of my mouth, I wrapped my arms around his neck. Alonso picked me up and threw my back against the door. Even with me into the kiss, the sound of the lock clicking could be heard.

I'm not having sex with you, Alonso, I silently spoke. Yet, for some reason I couldn't voice those words aloud. It was like, my body and soul wanted to feel him, but my mind and heart wasn't ready to feel him again. Not just yet.

When Alonso walked the short distance to the bed and laid me down, my breathing thickened as thoughts of that picture flashed in my head. The image of him laying in Nicole's bed hit me like a ton of bricks, as his confession of sleeping with her stung at my heart. My body tensed up and I knew he felt it because he slowly pulled back and asked was I okay. My head shook and my eyes watered up.

Slowly, Alonso sat up. As he was running his hands down his face while blowing out a deep breath, I sat up. By now, I had tears streaming down my face. *See?* This was the exact reason I had been trying to avoid him. I knew either I would start crying from the hurt and pain, or I would give in and take him back and let him have all of me. Sadly, I wished it was the taking him back part that consumed me right now. I was sick of crying, and I especially hated for him to know I was still crying over him.

Was this immature of me? I wondered.

"I'm sorry," I softly apologized as I wiped the tears from my eyes.

"Nah, shawty. I'm sorry. Don't apologize about some shit that you didn't do wrong." Out the corner of my eye, I could see his tongue run across his lips right before he turned around to look at me. "I fucked up, and I'm man enough to admit my fuck ups."

For a moment, we both remain quiet, lost in our own thoughts. While he stared at me, I looked down at my hand; at the ring he'd given me. I twirled it around on my finger. No guy had ever given me anything before, and for one to give me something so expensive meant so much to me. To me, it signified his love, but this ring just wasn't enough.

"I wanna forgive you, Alonso." I let off an exhausted breath as I brought my eyes up to look at him. "But, I can't. Like, as bad as I wanna forget what you did and make things the way it was, I... I just can't do that. Like, every time I look at you, I just see you laying in *her* bed. I know it might be childish, but..."

Alonso grabbed my hand and brought it to his lips. "How you feeling ain't childish, shawty." He paused to lick his lips. "But I don't want you to give up on us. I'm not saying that you have to forget the shit because I know that's shit will take time, but at least forgive a nigga. Let me show you that you don't have to worry about that shit happening again. Like..." He blew out a breath that held so much frustration in it. Then he went on to say, "You know I love the fuck out of you, Eliza, and that shit ain't gon' change."

"And I love you too, Lonso."

"Well why the fuck you acting like you can't be with me? Like you can't forgive a nigga? You said give you time, and I been doing that."

"Well, clearly it's not enough time, Alonso." I batted my eyes, trying hard not to roll them. I guess he thought because I was young, it would've been easier for me to forgive him and overlook what he'd done to me, or maybe he thought because I let him take my virginity the same day I found out about him cheating, shit was sweet. It wasn't and only caused me to hurt more to know I was that dumb over his ass to reward him with my innocence.

"Look, man. I leave to go out of town tomorrow. I'll be gone for a few days. Can you just take that time to think about what the fuck you want? If you don't want to be with a nigga no more, then let me know when I come back. I mean, it ain't gon' be no hard feelings, but just stop stringing me on."

"Stringing you on?" I frowned. "Oh, you mean like you did me?"

This time, Alonso scowl at me. "Aye, shawty, I didn't string you on. So what the fuck you talking about?"

"Um, lets see..." I threw up my hand and started counting. "You told me that you didn't want that bitch, but you ended up sleeping with her behind my back. You told me that you would never hurt me, but you did that when you cheated. You told me that you would never have me looking stupid, but you definitely did that. Need I go on?" In response, Alonso sucked his teeth and continued sitting there, looking dumb. "Exactly. So please don't sit there and act like you didn't play the fuck out of me."

"I didn't play you, but I know you'll never see it like that. So, all I ask is that you take the few days I'm away to get yo' fucking mind right." Getting off the bed, he had the nerve to say in a dismissive tone as he walked over to the bedroom door, "Be a fucking woman about the shit. If you don't wanna be with a nigga, then fucking say it."

I jumped off the bed as he was opening up the door, because he really had me messed up. Following him up the hall, I whispered-yell, "Oh yeah? Well, you should've been a fucking man and told me that you just didn't want to fuck me." As the words left my mouth, I pushed his ass in the back. I wasn't going to even lie, when he stopped walking and turned around to look at me with a hard scowl on his face, my ass got scared, thinking he was about to knock my ass out.

"Aye, don't put your damn hands on me, and why the fuck every-thing gotta be about fucking you? You that fucking desperate for some dick?" He uttered to me.

My bottom lip damn near hit the floor when he said that, and I couldn't even say shit. Mainly because I *was* acting desperate, but I didn't care because that was the way it seemed, like he just didn't want to have sex with *me*.

Even so, I said *whatever* as I rolled my eyes and walked around him. I wasn't crazy at all, and by the hard grimace that was plastered on his face, I knew he wasn't about to play any games with my ass. By now, I was ready to get the fuck away from him, and his damn house. Just as I got to the front door and was about to put my hand on the knob to open it, it opened and in walked Prince.

"Aye, bruh... Nicole just pulled up." Prince had a look on his face that spoke a million words. He knew it was about to be some shit once that damn girl saw me and Alonso walk out together.

"Man, I don't have time for this bullshit," Alonso said as he walked around me to go outside but stopped in his tracks from the dumb ass question Prince asked him. The negro had the damn nerve to ask Alonso did he need him to keep me inside while he went out there and handled Nicole. Before Alonso could even get anything out, my head shot around so fast to look at him, daring him to tell his brother, yes. Knowing better, he told him, "Hell fuck no. Nicole ain't about to do shit to her."

"Exactly!" I rolled my eyes at Prince and then followed Alonso outside, knowing he and my girls weren't about to let shit happen to me. But even so, I wasn't scared at all of Nicole, or anyone for that matter. The only person that would ever put fear in my heart was, Erika White.

"So this why my son can't get in touch with you, because you over here entertaining that young ass hoe?" Nicole started as she was walking in the yard. Alonso was already walking off the porch to meet her, to prevent her from charging at me while I walked out to the yard where Chyna and Zola were.

"Get in touch with me when? I just dropped AJ off at yo' mama's house. So, what the fuck is you talking about?"

"I'm talking about you putting this young, dumb ass hoe before me and your son."

I couldn't help but frown when she said that as I said to my girls, "This bitch is delusional." I was sure to speak loud enough for her ass to hear, just as she was doing, talking about me like I wasn't standing here.

"Nicole, what the fuck do you want, and where the fuck is AJ? Since he trying to get in touch with me, where the fuck is he?"

"Don't fucking worry about my gotdamn son. Clearly, he's not with you because you can't keep your head out that young ass bitch ass. You a poor excuse of a gotdamn daddy. Since you met this bitch, you don't—"

Alonso didn't even give her a chance to finish what she was saying because he knew what she was about to say, and he wasn't having it. Yoking her ass up, he told her, "Bitch, I'll break yo' fucking neck. Don't ever try me like I'm a fucking deadbeat. I been in my fucking child's life since day one. I don't know what the fuck your problem is, and I don't give a fuck, but don't even try me on that bullshit."

I honestly didn't blame Alonso for being that upset. Hell, even I knew his whole world revolved around AJ, and it was foul as hell for her to say that.

"Fuck you, Lonso. Fuck you and that young ass bitch!" Peeking around him, she looked where I was standing and push her attitude toward me, saying, "Bitch, you so fucking dumb. I guess that picture wasn't enough for you. Maybe I should've sent you a video of this nigga fucking me instead, huh? Dumb ass hoe!"

"Dumb?" I wasn't even about to let her embarrass me like that and I not say anything back, and I didn't care one bit if Alonso got mad or not. "Bitch, you the fucking dummy. You out here acting crazy knowing this nigga don't want yo' ass. You fucked and probably sucked him, but guess what, he *still* up this young ass bitch's ass while you trying to fight over a dick that's no longer yours. Now who's the dummy?"

When I called her out, she tried her best to get to me, but Alonso was right there to grab her. She was cursing and yelling, and I was too. I was sick of her bitter ass. Her trying to get to me got my girls rowdy as they tried to get to her. Clarence and Prince immediately grabbed Zola and I was scooped up from behind. It was so much going on that I didn't even see who had grabbed me, picked me up and carried me inside the house.

When I got inside, I was still fussing, and I noticed Chyna was too.

Clarence still had a tight grip on her, making sure she didn't go back out that door.

All of a sudden, the person that had me whispered, "Come on, shawty. Chill out. You too damn beautiful to be out here fighting." His soothing voice instantly calmed me. My body relaxed in his arms, but my chest remained heaving up and down. "Don't keep acting out of character over no man, shawty. That shit ain't a good look, especially when you above that."

Slowly, I wiggled out his arms, ready to turn around and see who was speaking those words to me. Other than Prince and Clarence, I didn't fool with anyone else out there in the yard. They were Alonso's friends, not mine, and everybody out there knew I was his. So, who in the hell was bold enough to compliment and remind me that I was above all the drama Alonso was taking me through was beyond the hell out of me. When I turned around, I was shocked to see that it was the brother that was in the car with Alonso the day I was fighting him, about that picture—*King*.

Licking his lips, he flashed a warm smile, raised his brow and asked me, "You good now?"

I didn't say anything because I was too pissed to. Not at him, but at Alonso—at my situation—all the bullshit I was going through when it came to Alonso and his baby mama. I wanted a sign from God and maybe this was that sign. If it was, it pissed me off because deep down, I really didn't want no sign. I just wanted Alonso in my life, but how could I be with him when his baby mama was forever trying to come between us. Automatically, my mind went back on what my mama told me: *while you trying to play grown like you ready for him, you better be ready for the bullshit that comes along with his ass.*

Right now, at this very moment, her word stung like a bee.

I was growing tired of Alonso and his bullshit, and I didn't even have the energy for any more of it.

13

Chyna Wilson

"This is some bullshit, and Lonso need to get his bitch in check," I stated as I jerked away from Clarence. Being that I had somewhat calmed down, he had loosened up his grip on me. "I need a damn blunt after this shit."

"Shawty, chill the fuck out. You act like this your battle to fight."

I couldn't help but frown when Clarence uttered that bullshit out his mouth. He knew damn well he would've been the same damn way had someone came at Alonso wrong, and I was sure to let him know that.

"When someone is trying to jump bad at one of my friends then it automatically becomes my battle, and if it was someone trying to fight your big head ass friend, you would be acting the same way. So what the fuck is you saying right now, because you talking out the side of your neck?" When he didn't have shit to say back, I said, "Exactly!"

"I'm so done with Alonso... I swear. I'm not about to keep going through this bullshit," Eliza fussed, making her way to the back of the house. The next sound heard was the bathroom door in the hallway, slamming shut. That's when Zola spoke up.

"See, that's what I was telling ya'll the other day. These niggas ain't shit." Clarence, Prince and the other guy in here with us all looked at her like she was crazy. Even I had to frown, not believing she had actually said that in front of her nigga.

In unison, they asked, "Fuck you mean niggas ain't shit?"

Then Prince told her, "If you feel that way then why the fuck you with me?" The look on his face said he didn't at all appreciate that shit, and I didn't even blame him. Zola knew she was wrong for saying that in front of that man, unless behind closed doors he was giving her a reason to feel that way—which it would've been hard to believe with the shit she was spitting at Eliza's house.

"Prince, you know I'm not talking about you. So please don't try and cause a scene," she tried fixing it up.

"Fuck that! You said all niggas ain't shit. You didn't single no body the fuck out."

Seeing where this was headed, I added my two cents by saying, "In her defense, she did single you out the other day when she said it. She claimed all niggas cheated, except you, because you didn't have a reason to."

"See? You know I wouldn't be talking shit about you, boy."

"And what the fuck you say when she said that bullshit?" Clarence wanted to know. He had taken a seat on the arm of the couch and had an unlit blunt in one hand and the lighter in the other, getting ready to spark it up. I didn't even want to feed his ego, so I lied and told him that I agreed with her. Yet, I was unable to contain my laughter, revealing it was a lie.

Zola even said, "Her ass was about ready to fight me, Clare, talking about some, not her boo."

The smile that coated his face caused my heart to skip a beat. My boo was so damn fine, and he had just gone and gotten his dreads retwisted, making him even finer. I just wanted to run my fingers through them while his head was in between my thighs. I swear, there was no greater feeling than that.

With a quick lick of his lips, he playfully flicked his lighter at me like he was about to set me on fire as he said, "You better had let her ass know."

"Oh, hush." I walked in between his legs, wrapping my arms around his neck. It was at the same time the front door swung open and in walked Alonso, looking pissed to the max, like he really had a reason to be.

"Where La-La at?" That was the first thing he asked. I just looked at him and didn't say shit, and neither did Zola. Clarence was too busy rubbing on my ass and kissing on my neck to say something, and Prince was still too pissed off at what Zola said. So, that left the other guy that was still inside, standing in the cut, minding his business—he was the one that answered Alonso by pointing to the back of the house. "Aye, ya'll. Let me talk to La-La for a minute. She'll be out in a minute."

"Nope. Hell no!" I quickly said. "I don't even think she wanna talk to you with the bullshit that just went down."

"Stay out my business, shawty."

"Ya'll put everybody in ya'll business just a few minutes ago!" I didn't know who Alonso thought his ass was, talking about some, stay out his business. How in the hell could he even say that when the whole damn hood was just in it? Maybe if he tamed his rachet ass baby mama, then me or anyone else would be in his damn business.

Slightly pushing me back, Clarence stood up, grabbed my hand and started pulling me to the door. He even told me, "Man, bring yo' ass on outside and let that man talk to his shawty."

"Tuh?" I rolled my eyes, still allowing Clarence to pull me outside. Before we walked out the door, I told Alonso. "I'm coming back in five minutes to check on her." In response, he walked toward the back of the house, leaving us to close the door behind us.

By the time we got outside and walked over to Clarence's car, I was caught up in some more drama, but this time, it was my own damn drama. Some thot bitch had the nerve to say to Clarence, "Oh, so this how you doing it, Clare?"

Instantly, I frowned as I turned to face her. I was still a little amped up from the altercation that'd just happened, so I spat smartly, "Clearly it is. And who the hell is you to be questioning my nigga?"

"I'm Selena, the bitch he's been fucking with the past few years, and the bitch whose house he was over the other night. You better ask about me," she spat, and Clarence immediately grabbed me.

"Well, bitch, you been replaced. As you can see, he's doing me now!" I smirked as I gave her a smug look, knowing not only that look, but what I had said got under her skin. I was pissed at the fact that whoever this bitch was had the nerve to step to me about my man, and claimed she was with him the other night. I wasn't saying Clarence was a saint, but I seriously doubted he would play with his life like that. "Clarence, let me go!"

"Man, you ain't about to be out here fighting this lying ass hoe. I be with you every gotdamn night, and you know that." He told me before turning his anger to her. "Aye, Selena, bitch you better take yo' lying ass on some gotdamn where before I let my girl fuck yo' ass up. You already know you can't fight."

"Your girl? Really?" She had the nerve to look me up and down. "Was she your girl when you were over here hugged up with me a couple of days ago?"

"Wait... I thought you just said he was at your house. Bitch, which was it? Either ya'll was hugged up over here, or he was at your house?" Okay, now I was a little pressed, for the simple fact that Zola had just told me a couple of days ago that Clarence ass was hugged up with some bitch. The part about him being at her house, I honestly didn't believe that, but the hugging part, I wasn't going to sit here and pretend I didn't believe that.

"Lil' girl, I don't have shit to prove to you. Anything you wanna know, ask yo' nigga." She then let out a laugh just as her sentence ended. "Well, I doubt that nigga will tell you the truth. You know how niggas are... They love to lie."

I gathered all my strength and pushed myself out Clarence's arms. Turning around to face him, I slapped the shit out of his ass, thinking about the night he'd come home messing with my allergy smelling like that stinking ass perfume. "So it was her stink ass perfume that I smelled on you the other night?" I grilled his ass.

"Stink?" The hoe repeated in an offensive voice. "Oh, nawl, baby.

That couldn't have been me if it was stinking, because I'm never that. Maybe it was another hoe he's fucking with."

"Yes it was her, Chyna, because I was here and—" Zola started but suddenly stopped talking. Quickly, I snatched my head around to face her so fast, remembering at Eliza's house she said she heard he was hugged up with some other bitch. Not once did she say she was here and had witnessed it with her own two eyes. That didn't sit right with me, because it meant if she was here and seen that, she damn sure didn't call me and tell me. Shoot, if I saw Prince and Alonso hugged up with some other bitch, I would call them after I beat that hoe's ass—but I guess Zola was cut from a different cloth than me.

Turning my attention back to Clarence, I shot daggers at him. Right now, what he had going on with that bitch was all that mattered.

"So this what you doing, Clarence?" I reached up and mushed his head. "You don't want me going back home, but you wanna be out here hugged up with another bitch?" I nodded my head up and down, indicating that I wasn't worried about it. I even added, "It's okay. Two can play that mothafuckin'—"

I didn't even get a chance to say, *game,* due to me getting hemmed up and thrown on the car.

"Two can play what?" Clarence roared. I didn't know what position he had me in, but my ass could barely move.

"Game, mothafucka. Two can play it."

"Yeah, alright. Try to play some mothafuckin' games with me if you want to, and watch I fuck you up."

My little self tried to throw him off me with my body, but he didn't budge, and that made me angrier. After what felt like forever, he gave me a quick peck on the lips before letting me up. I started swinging on his ass and cursing him out in Spanish, making sure I scratched him in his pretty little pecan buttered face. I wanted mothafuckas to know I, *Chyna Wilson,* had been there. "Oh, so you trying to show out. Huh? You showing out for this bitch?"

"Man, chill the fuck out. I'm not showing out for no damn body, girl." Clarence was backing back as he tried to grab my swinging arms. Every time he tried, I would move so he couldn't grab me, but I knew if he really wanted to stop me, he could. "Shawty, don't hit me no more. You going to make me beat yo' ass out here in front of—."

"In front of who? Your little girlfriend? I wish the fuck you would hit me!"

I had dealt with that bullshit a couple of years ago when I was with Spank, and I would be damned if I dealt with it now. With him putting his hands on me, or him cheating. But, as crazy as it might seem, deep in my heart, I honestly didn't feel like it was how Zola and the Selena bitch tried kicking it. Again, I wasn't saying Clarence was a saint, and I could be wrong, but I just didn't feel like *my nigga* would play me like that. I wasn't crazy, but over the years I had bossed up and I let him know over and over again that I would fuck him up if he cheated on me, and I was dead ass the fuck serious, too.

I might've been young, but I had learned a lot dealing with Spank, and the number one thing I'd learned was to never let a nigga think you will tolerate his bullshit. Well, that was number two. Number one was, I learned my worth.

"Aye, La-La, come get yo' crazy ass homegirl before I fuck her up." I turned toward the front door to see Eliza and Alonso walking out. I guess he depended on her to talk some sense in me since it appeared Zola wasn't going to do or say shit. Plus, she had just snitched on him, so I knew he wasn't going to say shit to her.

"Clarence, fuck you, dawg," I said as I threw up my middle finger at him. Turning around, I took one look at the bitch that thought it was okay to come try and start drama between my nigga and me. "And you, bitch, you lucky I don't beat your ass just for coming over here with that bullshit. If you come over here lying on my nigga again, I'ma fuck yo' ass up, and I put that on Clarence life."

"What? Shawty, you tripping." I just rolled my eyes as everybody else laughed. Pulling me in his arms, he leaned down and started kissing on my neck. "You know I like that crazy ass shit. I'm ready to take you home and beat that pussy up."

I laughed as I tried pushing myself out his arms, but he wasn't letting go as he told me he was dead ass serious. Because I knew ol' girl was looking, I wrapped my arms around his neck as I started kissing him. When I pulled back, I told him, "I have to take La-La home first. How about you ride with me. We can drop one of your cars off. We need to get something to eat anyways."

"Bet. Let me holla at my nigga and then we can leave." When Clarence walked off, I looked over at the Selena bitch. I smiled and winked before sticking my tongue out at her. *Childish?* So what? Nobody out here was going to check a bitch. She rolled her eyes as she gave me a funky look. Before she walked off, she told me to watch my back, and called me a hoe. I brushed her little threat off because there wasn't a hoe that put any type of fear in my heart.

"What the fuck did she just say?" Eliza walked over to me, grilling the girl as she walked out the yard. Her eyes were bloodshot, and I knew she had been in there crying. My heart went out to her.

"Girl, nothing! Bitches get pressed when somebody else is getting the dick," I yelled loud enough for her and everybody else to hear. "She lucky I let her slide, but that's the girl that Zola was talking about Clarence was hugged up with over here. I still don't think it's the way they tried kicking it, though." I didn't even bother telling her how Zola contradicted herself. I guess the day at Eliza's house, she didn't want to tell me that she was here when Clarence was entertaining someone else because me and her probably would've fought that damn day.

How could we be best friends and you not check my nigga after seeing him hugged up with someone else? And that further let me know that it wasn't at all how they were trying to kick it. Either that, or Zola wasn't really my friend.

"That's why I used to tell Alonso about having all these folks over here, but he's so stupid and will just let anybody in his yard. Now he got bitches over here trying to come at you sideways and shit."

"Girl, fuck that bitch!" Turning to look for Zola, she was sitting on the porch, looking down at her phone. I wanted to go up there and snatch it from her and ask her was she here when Clarence supposedly had been hugged up with Salena or what, but I didn't because I wasn't trying to cause a scene, but this was a conversation that we would damn sure revisit in private.

"Hey, you ready to go, because I know you're still not about to let Alonso drop you off at home, are you?"

"Hell, no. You can take me. I don't even want to say shit to him." Eliza looked over where Alonso was standing and frowned. "I'm sick of him apologizing on behalf of that hoe and promising he'll handle it. This is the last time I'm putting up with that, girl. I'm so done, and I told him that, too." Her voice was filled with much attitude, but the hurt being heard outweighed it.

All I could do was shake my head as Clarence was making his way back over to us. On the way to drop the car I was driving off at his house, I told Eliza that he was riding with me to take her home. Of course she was cool with that. After dropping the car off, Eliza and I jumped into his box Chevy with him and we left, heading to drop her off. She only lived about twenty-minutes away from him, so we got to her house in no time. After she got out, we went straight to IHop since the both of us was in the mood for some breakfast.

We were sitting in the booth waiting for our food when I blurted out, "Hey, was Zola at Alonso's house the other day? The day you were supposedly had been hugged up with—"

"Yeah, her lying ass was there..." Clarence cut me off. "And she knows damn well I wasn't hugged up with that damn girl. I don't know why she didn't tell you that shit instead of saying the bullshit she said. I guess she knew it was bullshit, too. That's why her dumbass stopped talking." I heard everything he was saying, but I wasn't paying attention because I was still stuck on the fact that she was there. But then I had to tell myself; maybe she just didn't want to get in it. Yet, I didn't at all feel like that was the case, because Zola's ass stayed in our damn business, and it wasn't sitting well with me that this one time she wasn't.

"Well, if you weren't hugged up with her, what really happened, Clarence? Why they say you was?" I asked that to get my mind off Zola. Clarence licked his lips and then dropped his head. When he brought it back up to look at me, I could tell it was something he wanted to say but at the same time he didn't want to. So, I asked, "What's up?"

Leaning over the table, he collapsed his hand together, looked me dead in the eyes and asked, "What niggas you let run a train on you?"

Clarence's question damn near knocked the breath out of my ass. Automatically, my chest started heaving up and down as my eyes batted. "What?" My word came out in just above a whisper. I had been with Clarence for damn near a year, and not once had he brought up that crap. At this very moment, I felt like I was going to lose him, and it caused tears to form in the pit of my eyes before making their way down my face.

"Shawty, what the fuck is you crying for?" Clarence asked, his voice laced with confusion and irritation, and although my head was down, I could still feel him glaring at me. When I didn't say anything, he let out a chuckle and then went, "And I didn't even wanna believe that bullshit when Selena said it."

That bitch!

This time, I had no other choice but to speak up. It was out there and as bad as I wish I would've been the one that had told him, I wasn't, and now was my chance to let him know the story behind it. In a mumble, I stated, "I was drunk."

Again, Clarence chuckled, and when I brought my head up, he was shaking his. "Drunk?" He repeated but didn't give me a chance to say anything in return. "You were that gotdamn drunk that you let multiple niggas fuck you?"

Just like before I felt disgusted with myself and judging from his voice, he was disgusted with me as well. But, what he said was the truth—I was so drunk that I allowed that to happen, and now, all I could do was continuously ask myself how in the hell could I had been so damn careless.

"I know. I've never gotten that drunk before, and that's why I don't drink like that anymore." Yeah, I know I was too young to be drinking in the first place, but that didn't mean I didn't have a few mixed drinks every now and then, at parties especially. I was living the fast life, but thanks to that horrible night, I had slowed down a lot. Well, that night and me meeting my boo. *Lord, please don't let this man dump my ass.* I prayed to myself. "I didn't want that shit to happen, Clarence, and I hate myself for even allowing shit to go down like that, for allowing them to videotape it..."

"What? Hold the fuck up?" The disgusted look that was once plastered on Clarence's face was replaced with a stone-cold hard ass frown. I didn't know if he was pissed at the fact that I let someone record me getting fucked by all those niggas or pissed at the person that had actually recorded it. "Nobody said shit about no damn video. So mothafuckas done seen that bullshit?"

I nodded my head as the waitress brought us our food. Right now, I was in no mood to eat. My appetite was gone, and I thought Clarence's was too until he grabbed his fork and started eating. The frown was still visible on his face, but it wasn't as hard as it was. After a few minutes of the intense silence, I asked, "You're going to leave me now, ain't you?"

For about thirty long ass seconds, Clarence didn't say anything as he continued eating, not even looking at my ass. Then, he finally hit my ass with, "I wanted to." Sitting his fork down, he leaned back in his seat and eyed me through intensified eyes. "Since I found out about that shit, I kept telling my fucking self that I didn't want to be with nobody that liked getting trains ran on them and shit—"

"But I didn't like that shit, Clarence!" I made clear. "I was drunk, and it only happened one damn time. There's no way I would've allowed that to happen if I was in my right state of mind. They knew I was drunk, and they took advantage of me." At this point, I was embarrassed and pissed off as I explained that to him. Not at Clarence or myself, but at Tyrell and the other two dummies that had taken advantage of my situation.

"Nah, shawty... You gotta take responsibility for your own actions. You keep saying you was drunk, so ain't no telling what bullshit you was on. I've seen you when you're drunk and how you be on my dick, you probably were ten times worse that night. And niggas ain't turning down no pussy." All I could do was suck my teeth and drop my head. "So, who was these niggas, and where the fuck were your girls at for this shit to happen?"

"I went by myself. La-La couldn't get out the house and Zola just didn't want to. I guess I should've just kept my ass at home too."

"Yeah, you should've." Throwing my back against my seat, I folded my arms over my chest and pouted like a five-year-old. "Now answer my other question."

I stared at Clarence as he eyed me back. "Just some boys I went to school with, and this was before you, Clarence, and I know that bitch only told you so you could break up with me. You know it too, that's why you never asked me until now."

"Nah, I didn't ask you because I didn't want to know the truth."

I blew out a long frustrating breath, ready to accept whatever Clarence was about to tell me. I prayed he wouldn't, but if he was about to break up with me over this, I was ready to accept it for what it is. "Well, you got the truth, so what you going to do with it?"

"Ain't shit I can do with it." He shrugged, grabbing his fork and started digging in my plate. "As long as that bullshit don't happen again, you stuck with my ass, shawty. Dead ass."

I had to bite down on my bottom lip to keep from smiling, loving the sound of that.

"Whatever..." I said, shyly. "And I know it might not be the right time to ask this, but who the hell was that bitch, anyways?" I didn't have to say Selena's name in order for him to know I was talking about her.

"Man, just some hoe I used to fuck with. I haven't fucked with her in months, though. And I wasn't even hugged up with that bitch. So, her and yo' homegirl was bogus as fuck for trying to kick it to you like I was—which, I expected that shit from Selena, but I don't want her ass and she knows that."

"Yeah, you better not want her ass." I pressed my lips together before a smile broke through. He licked his lips and smiled as well. It was insane how sexy this man—*my man*—was. Like, Clarence was everything to me, and he meant even more. No, we hadn't said the four-letter word—*love*—but I honestly felt the love was there on both ends. At least I knew it was on mine. I mean, how could I not fall head over heels in love with this man? He might not have verbally voice the words, but his actions showed a lot. Clarence had shown me so much love and affection than the ones that had actually said, *I love you*, to me.

Reaching over, he grabbed my hand that was resting on the table. Looking me dead in the eyes, he told me, "You know you the only one for me. I don't know what yo' lil' young ass did, but you got a nigga ready to settle down and shit."

My eyebrow rose. "Ready? You better already be settled down."

Clarence laughed and dropped his head when I said that. I guess he wasn't even thinking about what he'd just said, or how he'd worded it. "Man, you know what the hell I mean."

I cracked a smile. "Yeah, I know what you meant, boo. I was just fucking with you, and I feel the same way, Like, I know I'm young and everything, but I really see myself marrying you and growing old with you. Oh, and having plenty of babies by you."

"Plenty of babies, huh?" I nodded my head. "And growing old? You must be in love with a nigga?"

I let out an embarrassed chuckle, knowing my face had turned red that fast. His question caused a jittery feeling to settle in the pit of my stomach. Yeah, I was definitely in love with his ass, and felt silly about it like the signs of him loving me back wasn't there. My head dropped, unable to stand the way he was looking at me. He had his bottom lip tucked in his mouth and his eyes were penetrating, like it was searching for something deep within my soul.

"You know you don't have to be scared to tell me you love me, right?"

"And you don't have to be scared to tell me you love me, either" I snapped, playfully, rolling my eyes.

"I never said I was scared to tell you. You the one talking about spending the rest of your life with somebody and having babies and shit." I sucked my teeth, hating how he was putting me on the spot, and the fact that his voice was filled with humor only pissed me off as well as shamed me more. "You love a nigga, Chyna?"

A groan escaped my mouth. "Maybe, Clarence. Damn. Do you love me?" When he said maybe, I narrowed my eyes at him, causing him to laugh. Easing from his side of the booth, he came around to my side.

Clarence leaned over and started kissing on my neck, causing me to fight the urge of closing my eyes and moaning. His lips were so soft and felt damn good on my skin. When he got to my ear, he whispered, "Hell yeah I love you. I love the fuck out of yo' ass, and I can't wait to spend the rest of my life with you."

"And what about kids?" No, I wasn't ready to have none right at this moment, but I for damn sure wanted to have Clarence's kids.

"Hell, yeah." I felt his hand on my knee and trail up my thighs. Knowing where he was headed, I opened my legs, giving him full access to my pussy. I even reached over and put my hand on his dick. It was rock hard, but that was expected because I always turned his ass on. "If you want, we can go home and practice on it right now."

"Let's go." I was horny and wanted some sex, and that made me overlook him saying we could get started on the baby making. I had a goal I wanted to reach, and Clarence knew that because we'd talked about it. So I knew he wasn't trying to impregnate me right now. Yet and still, it wasn't going to change the fact that we were about to go home and make sweet love.

We'd just confessed our love for one another, so I knew sex this time around was about to be bomb as fuck.

14

Zola Mitchell

I sucked my teeth and rolled my eyes as I walked in the house behind Prince. I was so sick of him that I didn't know what to damn do, and even sicker that I had to pretend that I was still happy with his ass. I wanted to be free, but I knew I wasn't going to find another man that would provide and treat me as good as him, so, I was forced to stay in this relationship that I wasn't happy in.

"I know you're not still mad about what I said at your brother's house, Prince?" I frowned, walking into the bedroom where he was. While I had stopped by the kitchen to get me a drink of water, he headed straight to the bedroom. When I walked in, he was removing his shirt.

"I'm good, believe that!" He tried convincing me.

"You're not good! You didn't even say shit to me on the way home. You stopped and got you something to eat and didn't even ask if I wanted anything."

"You say niggas ain't shit, right?" Prince looked at me threw a raised brow. I thought he was really being immature right now, especially when we stopped at Burger King and he didn't think to get me something. I had to place another order at the window when he got ready to pay. His ass was acting childish over nonsense—over some shit that had nothing to do with him.

"I wasn't even talking to you, Prince, and you know that." When he said he didn't know a gotdamn thing, I yelled, "Well, I told you I wasn't talking about you."

"I don't give a mothafuck what yo' ass told me! You meant what the fuck you said. If that shit didn't apply to me, then you would've let it be known when you uttered the bullshit instead of me having to check you about it."

Check me? This mothafucka was dumber than I thought if he *thought* for one second that he had checked me.

I sucked my teeth as I threw up my hand. I wasn't about to go back and forth with him about this shit. If he wanted to be in his fucking feelings, then he was going to be in them by his damn self. "You know what... whatever. I'm not about to argue with you over this bullshit. I said what the fuck I said, and I told you that I wasn't talking about you, but you can think what you want to think." With that, I walked into the bathroom and slammed the door behind me.

I was sick of arguing with his ass every other day about nothing.

Inside the bathroom, I just stared at myself in the mirror, not even believing I was living an unhappy life all because of what a man could do for me. But, as that saying goes, if you can't be with the one you love, then be with the one that loves you—Or was that saying just the way I felt? I didn't know, but it was damn sure my current situation. I knew Prince loved me. From day one, he never hid how he felt about me. Even when we were mad at each other, he still made it a point to show me. Any girl would be happy to have a man like him, but he just wasn't it for me. I've tried to love this man like I knew he deserved to be loved, but I just couldn't give him my all.

The love I had for someone else stopped me from loving the one that deserved all my love. The one that desperately wanted my all. Don't get me wrong, I did a damn good job at hiding my true feelings for another man from Prince and everybody else, because the last thing I wanted anyone to do was judge me on the person that I was deeply in love with, my girls especially.

With a suck of my teeth, I took in all the air that I could muster up and slowly released it. Although I didn't want to, I knew the right thing for me to do was go back in there and apologize to Prince. I absolutely hated this part, when I had to apologize. Any other time, whether I started the argument or not, Prince would be the one saying sorry as if he'd done something wrong. However, this time I had a feeling that he wasn't saying it this time around, and as bad as I hated to admit it, I didn't blame him.

Opening the bathroom door, I saw that he wasn't in the room, so I headed up front. He wasn't in the living room either. Instead, he was outside on the balcony. Before I walked out, I rolled my eyes upwards, preparing myself to go out there and deal with him.

"Hey," I said once I got out there. He was sitting in one of the chairs, smoking a blunt and messing around on his phone, making it a point to not say shit to me or even look up at me. "Look, I'm sorry about what was said. I promise, I did not mean anything by what I said. I was just talking about your brother and them. He cheated on my girl and now Clarence got some bitch coming for my friend, when he was clearly hugged up with the hoe."

This time, Prince took his eyes off his phone to look up at me. He frowned and sat his phone on the table in front of him. "You know damn well that man wasn't hugged up with that damn girl. Why the fuck you lying on him?" He asked but didn't even give me a chance to reply back. "And as far as my brother goes, that shit ain't got nothing to do with you. You be so invested in their business that you can't even see that I ain't happy."

"What?" I frowned, looking at him like he had just lost his damn mind. No, I wasn't happy either, but it still hurt for him to actually voice those words. When or if we ever called it quits, I wanted to be the one that ended things, not his ass. "What do you mean you're not happy? So, I don't make you happy, Prince?"

"Cut the fucking bullshit, Zo. Yo' ass ain't happy either, but you just ain't woman enough to say that. I bend over backwards for your ass, and you still walk around here giving me your ass to kiss."

"I do not, Prince, and you fucking know it." He didn't say

anything. "You must got another bitch or something? I mean, it has to be something for you to come at me sideways like this."

This bitch ass nigga looked me dead in the eyes and asked, "Would it matter to you if I did?" I wasn't going to even lie, that shit almost knocked the breath out my damn body. Here I was, saying how I was unhappy with him and he wasn't the one my heart truly desired, but the minute he started talking out the side of his neck, it angered me beyond measures.

I took a step back. I had to because I was tempted to punch his ass in the face. Through a chuckle, I said, "I'll take that as a yes." He didn't say anything and that pissed me off more. "I been staying here for fucking months, and now you wanna come hollering you seeing another bitch! Who the fuck is she?" I yelled.

I didn't tell you shit. You just assumed from a question I asked." When he said that, he grabbed his phone and got up, heading back into the house. I was right behind him, demanding answers.

"So, all this time I been sitting here trying to convince people we have the perfect fucking relationship, you been cheating on me?"

"You been trying to convince a lot of mothafuckas a lot of shit, lately." I wasn't going to even ask what in the hell that was supposed to mean, because it was true. I had been trying to convince him that I was in love with his ass, knowing I wasn't, and trying to convince my girls that he and I were good—so fucking good that he didn't have a reason to cheat on me. Right now, I felt like shit and I knew they was going to rub this bullshit in my damn face, Chyna especially.

"Where the hell you going? You just going to pack yo' shit and leave?" I started grabbing his clothes, throwing them out the duffle bag he'd put on the bed. "You think I'm going to stand by and let you go lay up with another bitch? Not on my fucking watch!"

"Zola, get yo' dumb ass out the fucking way. Damn!" Prince pushed me so hard that I fell on my ass. Instantly, I started crying. It wasn't that I was hurt or anything, but I was pissed that he was trying to leave me. I was pissed that I was about to be right back to living with my parents. No, it wasn't anything wrong with that because I had just as much freedom with them as I had with Prince, but it was just the principle of the matter.

Slowly getting up, I walked up on him and hugged him from behind, resting my head on his back. "But I don't want you to leave. Whatever I did, I'm sorry. Please don't leave me for another woman." I didn't care how I looked or whether I meant the words or not, I didn't want him to leave. Not right now, anyways. I needed this man to continue providing for me until things worked out in my favors. "I love you, Prince."

When Prince's body stiffened, I released him long enough to step in front of him. I reached up and wrapped my arms around his neck as I stood on my tiptoes, placing my lips on his soft ones. This man was so damn good looking. He kissed good, fucked and ate me out like no bitch in the world matter to him but me, and he was a damn good provider. A part of me hated the fact that I couldn't love him right, but I just couldn't stop my heart from longing for someone else.

"I love you too, shawty..." It sounded like a *but* was behind that, but I wasn't even about to give him the satisfaction of uttering some more bullshit out his mouth. I covered his lips with mine as I unfastened his pants, letting them fall to the floor. I caressed his hardened dick through his briefs before pulling them down far enough to release it, never breaking the kiss. The funny thing about all this, even with him spitting that shit to me, his dick still got hard for a bitch.

"Can I taste you?" I mumbled against his mouth. Prince didn't waste no time taking a step back. As he looked me in the eyes, he ran his tongue over his bottom lip before tucking it between his teeth. *Damn he's sexy.* Dropping down to my knees, I didn't waste no time grabbing his dick and getting to work. The last thing I wanted to do was leave him space to change his mind on giving me some dick, or to think about another bitch. Hell, I didn't even want to give him a chance to say whatever I felt he was going to say after he said he loved me. "Mmmm." I moaned between slurps.

"Shhhhit... Damn, girl." Prince grabbed the back of my head as it bobbled back and forth. I looked up at him as he looked down at me.

There was so much shit being said through our eyes. He might've had a pleasurable look on his face, but his eyes spoke something else. Still, I kept right on pleasing him. I wanted to give him a reason to stay. A reason to have a change of heart about the way he was feeling about my ass at the moment. I needed this man in my life right now, more than he would ever know. "Fuck!"

When Prince took a step back, I knew he did that to avoid busting in my mouth, because he knew I hated that shit with a passion.

"Get up!" He said to me as he walked over to the bed. He laid down on his back, signaling he wanted me to ride his dick that was standing straight up. Of course, I did it. I rode that shit like there was no tomorrow, too. In a matter of minutes, he was filling me up with his semen. "Damn." He mumbled, caressing my lower back. Leaning down, I placed my lips on his and we shared a passionate kiss.

Listen, Prince might've said whatever bullshit he wanted and felt however he felt, but he couldn't deny the fact that he loved the hell out of my ass.

Still on top of him with my face close to his, I told him, "I'm really sorry for what I said at your brother's house. I swear I didn't mean it like that. I would never say you ain't shit, baby. You do so much for me and... and up until tonight, I had no reason to feel as if you're cheating on me. So of course I wouldn't have said you a, ain't shit ass nigga."

For a minute, he just stared at me, still running his hands up and down my back. Then, he licked his lips and spoke. "Do you know how bad a nigga wanted to fuck yo' ass up?"

I laughed when I really wanted to roll my eyes, knowing damn well he wasn't going to hit me. Leaning down while I was still smiling, I gave him a peck on the lips and asked, "So you forgive me?" My voice was low and innocent as I pouted.

He shook his head, no. I thought he was playing until he then went, "Nah, I don't forgive you. Why the fuck would I? You thought giving me some pussy and head would change the way I feel?"

I was stuck. I couldn't move off him or anything as I glared down at him. "So you do have another bitch, huh?"

Prince damn near threw me off him as he got up, leaving me still sitting on the bed.

"This ain't even about no other woman. It's about you. You and me, and I can't do this bullshit no more. Every other day it's an argument about something, but today when you said that bullshit, I knew it was time for me to bounce. I know you young and got a lot of growing up to do, but—"

"Wow... Well, right now you're the one that's acting like the young one, trying to run away from love. Look at you, you done packed your bags to go lay up with some other bitch."

"I'm not running away from love, I'm running away from the one that don't want my love, and I packed my fucking bags because I'm going out of town with my brother and Clarence. Did you forget I told you that shit?" I had totally forgot about that, but I wasn't going to tell him. "And I want you out my damn house by the time I get back, shawty. Like, dead ass. I don't want this shit no more."

"And where the hell I'm supposed to go?" I jumped out the bed and was over in his face with the quickness.

"I don't know, and I don't give a fuck, but I don't want you here." With that, his inconsiderate ass walked into the bathroom and slammed the gotdamn door in my fucking face.

Pissed would've been an understatement.

Hell, hurt was even an understatement right now.

And I couldn't believe the man that claimed to have so much love for me was putting me out like I was a piece of shit.

In my eyes, Prince was low down as fuck for this, and if he thought he was going to have the last laugh, he was sadly mistaken.

15

Eliza Brown

"Hey, I'm about to go to the store. Are you coming, or are you staying here?" My mama asked me. It was late Saturday evening, and I had been laying on the couch since I got up this morning. I didn't have anything to do but lounge around the house and watch LMN all day. Chyna was chilling with her family since Clarence was gone, and I hadn't talked to Zola. As a matter of fact, neither Chyna nor me had heard from her since the day at Alonso's house when all that shit went down.

"Yeah. Let me go slip on some clothes." I sat up and headed to my room to get dressed. Ten minutes later, I was walking out the front door behind my mama. On the way to the store, we made small talk. I even tried calling my girl Zola again, but like before, she didn't answer for me. We usually talked every day, so for us to not hear from her was strange to me. Chyna had told me that Prince had gone out of town with Alonso and Clarence, so I knew Zola was more than likely free. "Something is up with Zola. Like, she's not answering the phone for me or Chyna."

"She's probably just somewhere being hot in the ass." I rolled my eyes when my mama belittled my friend. I hated when she did that.

"Well, her boyfriend is out of town, so I doubt that's the case."

"Well, maybe she just doesn't want to talk to you then, La-La. Hell, ya'll talk all day and night, maybe she just wanted a break."

This time, I shook my head and said in a teasing manner. "Nope, that better not be the case, because we don't get no break from each other. Not when it comes to talking on the phone. I'm letting Chyna slide today because she is chilling with her family and I'm too busy worried about Zola."

My mama rolled her eyes this time. "Girl, I'm sure she is fine, La-La, and I'm pretty sure you'll hear from her tonight." I didn't say anything aloud, but to myself, I said, *I hope*, and it was like my mama had read my mind. She looked over at me and said, "Trust me, she's out being hot in the ass. That's all her and Chyna know how to do, and you starting to be just like them, La-La." I rolled my eyes upwards and blew out a deep breath, now regretting not keeping my ass at home. "I don't care how much you do all that, La-La. You know like I know, since you met that damn man you been doing the most. I'm surprise you ain't running the streets now. He must've realized you was too young for his ass?"

"When I'm with him, you have something to say, and when I'm not you have something to say. It's like I can't win for losing."

"Oh, please believe, you're winning right now. Shit." Taking her eyes from the road, she looked over at me and then added, "Look, I know you think I'm hard on you, La-La, but I just want the best for you. I know how hard it is raising a baby as a teen. Your dad was here true enough, but he also had to work to provide for us, so he was never home. His job and him chasing other women took up all his time, so I was always left alone, taking care of you and trying to maintain my grades at school. That shit is hard La-La, and I don't want you to end up like that. You really think that boy cares about you? He might be with some other woman when he's not with you. A grown woman at that."

I knew my mama's intentions weren't to hurt me by her lecture, but her words sliced my heart to pieces, especially when she said Alonso might've been with some other woman when he wasn't with me. It hurt so bad because the shit was true, but I couldn't tell her that. Once again, I didn't want him to be portrayed as that type—*a cheater*. When it came to Alonso and my relationship with him, I wanted my mama to be wrong so bad.

"Alonso isn't like that, ma." My words came out in a murmur. My chest was heaving up and down due to me desperately trying to keep my tears from falling. Here I was, trying to make him out to be so perfect when he was far from it.

"How the hell you know, Eliza?"

"Because I know him." At least I thought I knew him. Right now, my mama had this man down to the T, and I was embarrassed as hell to admit it. There was no way I could let her know she was right about him. Even if we didn't work out when it was all said and done, I prayed this truth remained hidden from her. Well, for right now anyway. When it was old and I was over it, I'd probably let her know she was right, but I knew it wouldn't be no time soon. "Ma, you don't like Lonso because of our age difference. You never met him or anything."

"And I don't want to. I don't want to meet no grown ass man that's doing a seventeen-year-old." Her voice was dismissive, letting me know that was the end of the conversation. By now, she was shutting off the engine to her car and opening her door. "Are you coming in with me?"

I shook my head, no. I was in my feelings right now and just wanted to be alone. My feelings were hurt, and I was ashamed that I'd given this man all my love and he pretty much shitted on my heart and me. I hated Alonso for that.

While inside, I called Zola for the umpteenth time before calling Chyna. Unlike Zola, she answered. "Hey, boo. What's up?"

"Girl, nothing. Why Zola's ass still not answering the phone? Have you tried calling her?"

"Yup, and she didn't answer for me either. If I don't hear from her later on today, I'm going to her mama's house to see have she heard from her. This is so not like her."

"I know right, but I haven't tried to call her since you told me she was answering for you. Girl, Zola is on some fake shit."

"What?" I frowned, removing the phone from my ear to look at it. "What you mean fake shit, Chy?" I was shocked to hear Chyna say that. As far as I knew, we were always real with each other, so I couldn't help but wonder where in the hell this was coming from. "What's going on?'

"Girl... I'll tell you about it later. I'm going to come over your house later on and tell you everything."

Although I wanted to know now, I settled for her coming to my house later on. When I told her to call before she came, we ended the call. I was still lost and wondering how in the hell Zola, one of our besties were on some fake shit. I got lost in my thoughts and suddenly, I heard a light tap on my window, startling me.

"My bad, shawty. I didn't mean to scare you," the person standing there said. When I saw who it was, a surprised frown washed over my face as I opened the door instead of letting down the window to see what the hell he wanted.

"You scared me," I told him. He was grinning—flashing a sexy ass smile at that. I didn't even know how attractive he was until now, and it caused me to unintentionally bite down on my bottom lip. I didn't even know where that came from, but I straighten up real quick and said, "King, right?"

His smile widened. King was a dark-skinned cutie, with some deep ass dimples. He had it going the fuck on and was the total opposite of Alonso light skinned ass. My baby had it going on as well, though. They both were fine as hell in their own way.

Through a chuckle, he said, "Damn, I'm surprised you even remember me." He paused to run his thick tongue over his lips. "Every time we met you was either laying hands on somebody or getting ready to." I let out an embarrassed laugh as I dropped my head. He was right, so I had every reason to be embarrassed right now. "I'm glad that's not the case this time. You must remember what I said the other day?"

"Um, no. What you say?" I said in confusion, but of course I remembered. How in the hell could I not remember someone telling me that I was above all the bullshit I was going through? I guess in a way I just wanted to be reminded again.

King chuckled, like he knew I was lying. Then, he bit down on his bottom lip as he leaned forward then whispered, "I said you're too beautiful to be out here fighting, and don't keep acting out of character over no man, shawty. I don't care who it is, you above that shit."

I couldn't help but blush. "Thank you."

"There's no need in thanking me, shawty. I'm just speaking the truth."

"Yeah, and there's nothing wrong with speaking the truth, but sometimes we all just go through stuff, you know."

"That might be true, but when you're going through bullshit like that, it's time to remove yourself." For a minute, I couldn't say shit as my mouth twisted from side to side, knowing this man was speaking the truth. "And please believe, I'm not trying to hate on yo' boy, but I'm just speaking straight facts."

"My boy? Ya'll not friends?"

"Yeah, we're cool. I fuck with Lonso the long way, but regardless of how cool we are, when I see some shit I don't like, I speak on it, and I don't like the way he got you out here looking and acting."

"You saw me act out two times and now you think you know what's going on with Alonso and me." I tilted my head to the side as I continued looking up at him. "Unless you know something I don't know, for you to not like the way he got me out here looking."

Ugh. Why am I still trying to defend this man? I might not have been fighting every Felicia, Sabrina and Trina, but he did have me looking stupid with the altercations I'd had with his baby mama and the one time I had to swing on his ass. Yet and still, my dumb ass was standing here trying to justify shit.

Letting out a chuckle, King's head shook as he said, "I don't know shit. I'm just going by what I saw, but it seems like you got this shit all figured out, Lil shawty, so excuse me if I overstepped my boundaries." With that, he walked off, leaving the scent of his cologne lingering behind.

I just stood here watching him for a few minutes before turning around to get back in the car. However, I didn't get a chance to get back in because the sight in front of me prevented me from doing so.

"Zola!" I yelled, and my voice was laced with much attitude. She was on the next row over, walking towards the entrance. She stopped walking and looked in the direction my voice had come from. When she spotted me now making my way over to her, she whispered something to the person she was with and started walking my way, meeting me halfway. "What in the hell you doing with Tyrell?" I questioned, wondering if this was why Chyna said she was on some fake shit.

"I just ran—"

"You didn't just run into him, Zo." No, I didn't see them pull up together or her get out the car with him, but I wasn't buying the crap she was about to utter out her mouth. "So please don't say you just ran into him."

She rolled her eyes as she let out an irritated breath, like I was getting on her nerves. "Fine, I rode here with him, La-La."

"So, this why you haven't been answering the phone for me and Chyna? Because you been with him?" My face was contorted into a hard grimace, not knowing how to feel about this. She was with Tyrell. Tyrell of all people, and while Prince was out of town. This wasn't a good look, at all.

"No. If you must know, I lost my phone. Prince put me out and I lost my fucking phone."

Now, I was frowning in confusion. "Why did he do that?"

"Because he is fucking evil, La-La!" Zola yelled. Her eyes watered up as her bottom lip trembled. "All this fucking time I been thinking we had the perfect relationship; he's been cheating on me. He told me that he was unhappy, and he wanted me out his house."

"Zola, why didn't you tell us? Did you move back in with your parents?" I was shocked to hear this. I mean, my girl bragged on her man and threw in me and Chyna's face how good her relationship was and how her man didn't have to cheat, and now look at her ass. But I wasn't the one to throw shit in her face, so I just stretched my arms and told her, "Come here."

I tried pulling her in for a hug, but she shook her head and took a step back.

"No. I don't want you to feel sorry for me, because it is what it is, and I didn't call to tell you because you were having problems of your own, crying over your cheating ass nigga." My eyes bucked. I got that she was in her feelings right now, but all that was uncalled for. Yet and still, I just let her have it. "And I wasn't telling Chyna because she wasn't going to do shit but compare it to what she went through with Spank, and you know how she loves throwing shit back in my face. I don't have time for none of that bullshit right now."

"That's not true, Zola. We tell each other everything—"

"Yeah, well this one time I didn't want to tell ya'll anything. I had just said all niggas weren't shit, except my nigga and look where that got me. I been trying so hard to get ya'll to see that Clare and Lonso didn't deserve ya'll that I was getting cheated on myself. I'm sick of looking out for ya'll when nobody looks out for me."

By now, I was beyond taken aback. How in the hell was she upset at us about something we had no idea of?

"Zo, this is bullshit! I get that you're upset about what's going on with you and Prince, but there's no reason to take it out on us, like we would judge you. Like you said, I'm going through something, so I have no room to talk. When have we not confided in one another, regardless of what it is?" I paused, thinking she would say something, but all she did in return was roll her eyes and look the other way. "We tell each other everything, whether it's good or bad. Come on now. Why are you doing this?"

I just didn't understand what was going on right now. Zola was flipping this on me, like Chyna and me had done something wrong. I was beyond hurt and pissed.

"So, what are you going to do? Is this why you're hanging with Tyrell, because you didn't want us to know you and Prince aren't together?"

"No this not why I'm hanging with Tyrell, La-La. Damn. Can I have friends outside of you and Chy?"

"Friend? So ya'll that cool now?" Okay, at this point I had to laugh at her, because my girl was on some other shit. "Zola, you bugging out right now. Like, what's really going on? Did me or Chyna do something to you, or something?"

She was acting like she had it out for us for some reason, and I didn't like it one bit.

Instead of answering my question, she hit me with, "Look, I need to go ahead and get inside the store. I'll talk to you some other time." With that, Zola walked off, leaving me standing here in disbelief. I was so confused as I continued watching her until she had vanished, wondering what in the hell her deal was. Not only that, but when the hell she and Tyrell had become friends.

Zola knew we didn't fuck with him for what he had done to Chyna, and for her to be hanging with him was a violation. We were best fucking friends, almost like sisters, so that was strange. This man had taken advantage of Chyna when she was vulnerable, and for him and his stupid friends to video her at her lowest was beyond fucked up.

Now Zola had me looking at her sideways. Yes, we spoke to Tyrell at school or whatnot, but hanging with him was a whole different level of disrespect, especially knowing how the train and video effected our girl.

"Wow..." I whispered to myself as I turned around to see that my mama had made it to the car and was putting the groceries in the trunk. I motioned to take a step her way, but I was pulled back from behind, by the hair.

"Yeah, bitch, I told you Lonso wasn't going to always be around to protect you. Talk that shit now... You ain't got your girl here to back you up."

Nicole...

Just as the words left her mouth, I felt her fist connect to my jaw.

"Ahhh..." I yelled. I was so caught off guard that it took me a minute to actually start swinging back.

Here we were, standing in the middle of the parking lot, fighting. While she was yelling and cursing me out, I was yelling for her to let go of my damn hair that she still had a hold of from when she grabbed me from behind. Yeah, she was pulling my hair and raining punches on my ass, but I was still holding my own. Even when we fell to the ground and she was on top of me, I was swinging, making sure my fist connected with her face.

Somewhere along the way, she started getting the best of me, but that didn't last long before her body was being yanked off mine.

"Bitch, I don't know what the fuck you thought!" *My mama's voice.* Hearing my mama yell that out caused me to smile on the inside as I jumped up. My fucking face was throbbing, but I wasn't about to stand by and let my mama fight my battle. My mama was getting the best of that bitter ass bitch, too, and I didn't miss a beat as I grabbed Nicole's hair from behind and started pounding my fist against her head.

"Oh, so ya'll hoes tryna jump!?" Nicole yelled, still fighting back.

Everything was happening so fast that I couldn't even begin to tell you what all curse words were being said. I just knew right now, at this point and time, my mama didn't care that I was using them in front of her.

The fight seemed like it lasted forever until we all were being parted. It was a huge crowd that surrounded us, but it wasn't the bystanders that broke us up. It was the police, and I just knew one of us was about to go to jail. I prayed it was Nicole because she was the one that had initiated the fight.

"Break it up!" One of the policemen yelled. While Nicole was still trying to get to me, my mama was trying to get to her. *Me?* I was still in the police hold, trembling and scared to death that my mama or me was about to go to jail.

"These hoes just jumped me, and I'm fucking pregnant. I bet ya'll asses go to jail!" Nicole screamed in rage as she was told to shut up again before she went to jail. That got her ass quiet. My jaw damn near hit the ground by her words.

Pregnant? I repeated to myself as if I didn't hear her correctly.

When the police separated her from my mama and me, my mama asked, "What in the hell is going on, Eliza? Why the fuck am I out here fighting some bitch for beating your ass?"

"Ma, I... I... I don't..." I broke down. The police were asking me questions, but I was afraid to tell him that all this was over a man—a freakin' man that my mama forbidden me from seeing.

As I swallowed hard and was about to confess to everything, one of the cops that was over attending to Nicole walked over to us. He pulled the police that was in our face to the side. For a minute, I thought we was off the hook until they stepped back to us and one said, *Mrs. White, Miss. Brown, you both are being arrested for disturbing the peace and disorderly conduct,* my heart damn near dropped to my stomach.

One of them grabbed my mama, and the other one grabbed me, turning us around. My mama didn't say a word as she scowled at me with tears trickling down her face. All I could do was dropped my head, unable to look at her as both of the polices said at the same time, "You have the right to remain silent..."

As I was being cuffed, all I could think was, if this wasn't a sign to leave Alonso Davis alone, then I didn't know what was....

To Be Continued...

CPSIA information can be obtained
at www.ICGtesting.com
Printed in the USA
LVHW041629140820
663221LV00004B/814